The Pit Bull Wizard

Volume One: Animals of Asgard

by Brenda Sugar

ISBN: 978-1-966954-75-0 (paperback)
ISBN: 978-1-966954-76-7 (hardcover)
ISBN: 978-1-966954-77-4 (epub)
Library of Congress Control Number: 2025918307

"May the wonders of magic be with you"

Merlin

Prologue

My first memories are of a dark cold room and a lot of cages. The sound of dogs barking and puppies crying, and the unforgettable smells that comes from dogs using the bathroom. But the worst was the smell of death. I was born in a puppy mill. A puppy mill is a large-scale commercial dog breeding facility where profit is given priority over the well-being of the dogs.

The dogs live their entire lives in small wire cages with no human companionship, toys, or comfort, and little hope of ever becoming part of a family. They are bred without consideration of genetic quality, this produces generations of dogs with unchecked hereditary defects. I was born in one of those very small cages along with a brother and a couple of sisters. There wasn't room for any of us to move around much. There were a lot of other cages underneath us, on top of us, and next to us in the same situation, small cages with a mother and her puppies. We all huddled together to stay warm. My mother would cry and tell us, "This is not the life I want for you, just as it wasn't the life I wanted for my babies before you."

I didn't understand at the time what she was talking about and just to listen to her would give me chills and a strong sense of fear. We are guarded by an animal that has a thick, coarse brown fur with short legs and low profile. His head appears pointed and small for his body along with long claws on the front feet for digging and defense. He has short ears and a short, furry tail. There is a gland at the base of his tail that stores a stinky liquid that is just as powerful as that of a skunk. I soon learned his name is Turbo and he is a Badger.

It is Turbo's job to keep us all afraid. He'd stand up on his hind legs and point those long claws at our cage and is able to lift it up in the air and then let it fall without ever coming near the cage. Turbo can also talk to the humans that are running this puppy mill in a language they understand and Turbo understands them. He can talk to us too so we can understand what he is saying. He gets pleasure about coming over and staring into the cage showing his teeth as he grins at me saying through clenched jaws, "What are you looking at?" As soon as he would start talking I could feel the hair on my back stand up and I would begin to shake. He'd laugh at me when he would see how scared I was and say, "You are never going to survive where you're going. They should just kill you now." My mom would turn to look Turbo directly in the eye and say, "Get away from him Turbo, and leave him alone. When I get out of this cage, we'll see who's scared."

Turbo replies, "That's impossible. You will never get out of that cage. Over my dead body."

My mother snaps, "If that's the way it has to be then fine, over your dead body it will be." She then lifts her paw and moves me away from Turbo. Once he can no longer see me, he turns and walks to the other cages to continue his reign of terror with the other mothers and pups.

I remember curling up next to my mother and eventually falling asleep listening to her breathe. I used to dream about a place where there were big trees, green grass, and enough room to run as fast as I can. In my dreams, there are bunnies eating the grass and lying in the sun. I've never seen a bunny, I can just imagine what one looks like from the stories my mother would tell. There are also two figures in the dream, dogs I think but different from me. Off in the distance I can see a great white Husky watching me. I can feel her concern. All of a sudden her ears come up. I can see the hair on the back of her neck stand straight up and with a swoop of her tail she is gone.

I wake up startled.

One minute I am lying with my brother and sisters next to my mother and the next thing I know I'm being picked up by the scruff of my neck by something and it was like someone said, "Abracadabra." All of a sudden I am in an unknown place. It's very bright, so bright it hurts my eyes and I have to squint and a very warm light breeze is blowing. I am being carried over to a large odd-shaped metal building where whatever has me puts me down on a soft pile of dirt. I turn around to look at whatever or whoever is carrying me to this place and start trembling as I don't know this dog and my family is gone. There stands the big white Husky with piercing blue eyes that was in my dreams. I see blood running down her front right leg. I think to myself *that must be where Turbo's 'snap' hit her as we were leaving*. An even bigger question is how this Husky went from my dreams to be standing right in front of me?

Chapter One

The Escape

Turbo hears the commotion and comes running to the cages where we are all locked up. The door to our cage is open and for a brief moment Turbo sees this large Husky grab me with her teeth by the scruff of my neck and we both disappear. Right before we disappeared I see Turbo stand on his hind legs and point his long claws at the Husky. There is a snap and the Husky whimpers but continus to have a strong grip on me. My mother is in a panic and going into defense mode, showing her teeth, growling and crouched down ready to fight. She is trying to get her pups behind her after seeing me being taken away. My mother sees that the door to our cage is open and that Turbo is gone. My mother starts carrying my brother and sisters out of the cage and hides them before Turbo returns.

Turbo is very angry regarding what just happened. Things happened so fast that the last thing Turbo sees is the Husky grab me. He doesn't see that my mother is no longer in her cage and that her remaining puppies are gone too. Turbo goes and gets the humans that are running the puppy mill to show them what has happened. The short round human known as boss man has no hair on his head and markings all over his face and arms becomes very angry at Turbo for letting this happen and turns and punches Turbo in the face so hard it sends him flying across the room, crashing into some of the other cages that has dogs in them causing them to fall to the ground. Now all the dogs are barking and whimpering as their cages are falling upside down and sideways. The boss man yells, "Shut up before I get my gun and shoot every last one of you." The barking stops but low whimpers can be heard from those who are hurt during this incident.

The boss man and a female with greasy kinky curly long brownish hair who also has drawings on her arms walks over to where the empty cage is and doesn't see my mother or my siblings anywhere. Now the boss man's face is very red and he is screaming, "Find those puppies and that mother. They have to be around here somewhere."

The woman and Turbo are looking frantically behind the cages and under cabinets, in between boxes and behind doors. They both finally walk into a room off the big room from where all the dogs are kept and that is where they find my mother crouching in a dark corner with her puppies behind her.

The women yells, "Here they are. We found them." The man tells the woman to grab my brother and sisters and take them away from my mother even though they are way too young. The boss man with no hair on his head has a big heavy chain that he wraps around my mother's neck and puts her into an even smaller cage, then runs the heavy chain through the bars on the cage and puts a heavy lock on it. He turns to my mom and says, "Turbo will take care of you later."

He tells the female to take my brother and sisters to the other room where there is this big smelly man waiting. He also has drawings all over his face and arms with things sticking out from his lip and ears. He looks at the puppies and then at the female and winks. This causes the female to smile, showing only a few rotting teeth. The boss man sees this and with an open hand slaps the female on the back of the head and tells her to give him the puppies and wait for him in the other room. She walks off as the big smelly man says, "These will do just fine, we will train the boy to fight or use him for bait. And as for these females, I will use them for breeding." He hands the boss man some money, puts my sisters and brother in a small box and takes them with him.

The boss man puts the money in his pants pocket then returns to the room where all the dogs are and says to Turbo while pointing at my mother, "Get rid of her. She is no longer good for breeding. Look at her, she is all worn out and I doubt that she could even carry a liter. I'm not going to waste time and energy trying to breed her again." With that the boss man unlocks my mother's cage, takes off the lock to the chain and hands the chain to Turbo. The boss man then grabs the cage and dumps my mother on the ground. Turbo turns to my mother and says, "It will be a pleasure to get rid of her master." Looking straight into my mother's eyes he continues, "You may think your son got away but we will track him down and find him." He goes on saying, "As for the dog that took him, she will pay with her life for stealing him from us."

Turbo starts pulling on the chain that is around my mother's neck, dragging her. She is so weak and her legs are stiff from being locked in that tiny cage. She is not able to stand and walk. Tears are running down her face as she tries to remember how she got here in the first place. Turbo is losing his patience with her and starts to pull on her even more. The chain is getting tighter around her neck, she lets out a cry from the pain. Turbo turns to look at her and begins to laugh. He says to her, "Soon your pain will be gone along with your worries about your pups."

He continues to drag her causing the fur to start rubbing off her entire left side and her legs. He then says to himself, "This is the part of my job that I really enjoy." He sniffs the air and a smirk comes over his face and turns his head back to look at her and says, "Is that blood I smell? Hey you back there, momma pit, is that your blood I smell?"

Turbo continues to drag her and comes across a very dark wooded area. Turbo says to himself, "I really don't have the time to deal with this dog." He turns back to look at her and continues, "She looks almost dead right now anyway. What harm could come out of me just leaving her here to die on her own?" Turbo says to my mother, "It's your lucky day. I'm not going to kill you, I'm going to just leave you here. Maybe you will get lucky and someone will come along to help or maybe not." Turbo walks up and takes the chain from around my mother's neck, turns and walks away dragging the chain behind him.

My mother is just lying there trying to catch her breath and says in a whimper, "I wonder, I hope someone will come along to help me. I wonder what is going to become of me and my puppies. What happened to Merlin?" As she lay there she hears voices. She says to herself, "I need to make some noise to get their attention, but what if they're bad? What difference does it make if I don't get help? I'm going to die anyway!" She starts to let out a whine but nothing comes out. She lays there and takes in a few deep breaths and let's out a whine so loud it echoes.

There is a couple walking down the street and the female says, "Did you hear that?"

The man replies, "Yes and I think it came from over there."

They start walking in the direction that they think they heard the sound coming from. My mother hears them coming and cries out again to make sure they find her.

As the couple turns the corner they see a very badly beaten wounded female Pit Bull lying there almost dead. They approach her and she is able to raise her head. The female says, "Look she's alive."

They get closer to her and the female says, "She looks like she just had pups."

The male replies, "You can bet those pit bull pups are long gone. She looks like she has had a pretty rough life, probably the product of a puppy mill." He turns to the female and says, "Go get the car. I'll wait here with her. We need to get her to a vet immediately or she IS going to die."

The female runs off to get the car. The male sits down at the dog's head holding her, petting her and at one point bends down and kisses her on the forehead. The entire time he is talking to her and telling her to hang on and that they are going to get her help and do everything they can to find out who did this to her and hopefully find her pups, but she needs to just hang on.

She lays her head down in his lap and closes her eyes knowing she is now with people who were going to take care of her, waiting for the female to return with the car. Suddenly she cries out, with her head still in his lap and says, "Yes, we need to find my pups." All the male hears is the crying though, and holds her even closer and whispers, "You're going to be okay."

Chapter Two

Uncontrolled

A woman is standing at the kitchen sink that looks out toward the Quonset, a lightweight prefabricated structure of corrugated galvanized steel that has a semicircular appearance and comes in all different sizes. There are things stored in there that I have no idea what they are or what they are used for. I sit there for a while just basking in the sun trying to figure out where I am, where my family is and how I got here.

After a while I see this woman walking down to another building that has horses and cows. She is wearing jeans, a sweatshirt and boots. She has strawberry-blond hair that is pulled back in a ponytail. Her face appears sad, but also kind. Following right behind her are those other two figures that I have seen in my dreams: dogs, big dogs. I'm keeping my eye on her since I don't know who she is. I sit for what seems like forever, then I see her coming out of that building. I try to move back out of her sight but instead catch her attention. Now she is heading my direction and those two big dogs are with her. I decide to try and act tough to scare them away and start barking. That doesn't work either. The one dog grabs me by the scruff of my neck and picks me up.

The lady says, "Makayla bring him to me." Makayla a German Rottweiler walks over to the lady and as she gets closer to me, holds out her hands and

Makayla gives me to her. The next thing I know, she has me in her arms, and is giving me kisses, and says, "Where did a little guy like you come from? I'm sure you didn't get here on your own."

She says to herself, *surely no one brought a tiny puppy out here and dumped him. I know this is a favorite place for city folk to bring animals they don't want, but a puppy? What's wrong with people?*

She is now holding me up in the air and says, "I can't imagine anyone not wanting you." I start to whine and she sits me down and I run off to the bushes with both Makayla and the lady right behind me. I find a bush and let it rip: diarrhea. She sees this and says, "Oh no, this isn't good. I need to get you to the vet's and I hope you don't have Parvo, little guy.

Now I am in a moving thing she refers to as a truck. It moves and I just have to sit there . We arrive at the Spring Living Vet Clinic and Dr. Jennifer starts doing tests on me. She sticks needles in my leg and a stick up my butt. I did not like that at all and let out a yelp as loud as I can. When I did this, the lady that brought me here picks me up, holds me in her arms and starts rubbing my back and head.

Dr. Jennifer comes back in and says, "Good news: he doesn't have Parvo, but he does have worms and a lot of them. We will give him some medication now to start to get rid of them and will send you home with medication to continue for seven days. He is also very dehydrated so he will need electrolytes during those seven days as well. He is very young, can't be more than 4 weeks old. Where is his mother?"

The lady holding me replies, "I don't know, I found him out in my Quonset."

Dr. Jennifer shouts, "Are you telling me that someone just dumped this puppy on your property?"

The woman replies, "I don't know what else to think."

Dr. Jennifer says, "I'm sure he is not going to have one but let me check him for a chip just in case." Dr. Jennifer walks out the door and when she returns, she has this strange looking thing in her hand that she uses to swipe down my back. Dr. Jennifer says, No chip. It was worth a shot. She looks at the lady holding me and says, "It looks like you are now the guardian of a little purebred red-nosed Pit Bull. What are you going to call him?"

The lady says, "For some reason I am hearing in my head the name Merlin, maybe he's a wizard. Merlin the Pit Bull Wizard." She smiles. "He is going to be just fine. Makayla is already playing momma to him but I don't know how Rocky is going to take it."

Makayla does take care of me just like I think my own mother would have had she been here. In fact I would almost think Makayla is my mother except for the fact that she is a Rottweiler. She gives me baths, lets me climb all over her, chew on her ears. Whatever I want, Makayla lets me have.

Then one day Makayla is no longer around. I run around the property looking everywhere for her. Then I pick up on her scent and follow it. Her scent takes me to the back of my guardian's truck. I jump up on the bumper and start scratching at it trying to get it to open. I then start barking really loud to let her know that I'm here. About that time my guardian catches up to me and picks me up. She cries, "Merlin, Makayla died. I don't know what happened. I came home and found her on her bed over there. I thought she was sleeping but she's past away."

I squirm so she will put me down. Just then Rocky comes up to me and licks my tears. He puts his paw on mine and lets me know that he is there and things are going to be okay. That's when I also notice another faint smell, one that takes me back to the puppy mill. That scent is from a Badger by the name Turbo. I think to myself: *was Turbo here? Is he responsible for my Makayla's death?*

A couple days later, my guardian gets a call from a shelter that another shelter is getting ready to destroy a female Rottweiler. The shelter lady says, "I know you just lost Makayla, but this girl needs someone who is good with Rottweilers and knows how to handle them." This is how Miracle came to be part of our family.

I have now been at the Sugar Ranch for six months and have my two best friends: Rocky, a half Rottweiler and half Shepherd mix and Miracle, a German Rottweiler. I still think about Makayla and miss her very much. My guardian says that one day we will be together again at Rainbow Bridge, wherever that is, but my guardian says it will be a while.

I have a routine now where I get out of my crate that sits next to my guardian's bed every morning. It has a bed inside of it and a blanket with horses on it. I like to rearrange my blanket but then my guardian just comes back and folds it back up again. I don't have to have the door on my crate closed anymore because I stay in my crate all night.

Rocky sleeps in my guardian's room too, on a bed at the foot of my guardian's bed and Miracle sleeps in the mudroom where she has a bed.

After we all wake up, Rocky and I stop at the mudroom to get Miracle. Our guardian is standing at the front door, holding it open for the three of us to go outside for a run. These days it is starting to have a chill in the air and I can see my breath. There is even some frost on the trees and grass. I don't like the cold. My fur is short and doesn't keep me very warm and I hate the cold on my paws. I hear my guardian talking about getting me a coat to wear when I go outside, I just hoped it's not one of those goofy ones like I see on TV.

As I run down past the barn I see the horses sticking their heads out of their stall and I can see icicles hanging from their chins and their fur is frosty. The grass is cool on my paws so I start to run around the pine trees. While we are outside my guardian is getting our breakfast ready. Sometimes she will have some cinnamon rolls baking in the oven. I don't get any of them but they make the air smell so good that I do drool a bit. If I am lucky, while she is eating one, a piece will fall and I will be right there to snatch it up.

Before going back inside to eat when my guardian calls me, I have to run down and check on the rabbit family that lives under the tool shed. The shed sits a ways from the front of the house and low enough to the ground that most predators couldn't get under there. There is also another family that lives under the deck, but they just moved in there and don't quite trust me yet so I just leave it up to them when they want to trust me. Since there are snakes out there that love to eat rabbit, I just feel better to check on them and know everyone is okay. Now that it is getting colder, they won't have to worry about snakes for a while.

As I approach, I let out a bark so they know it is me approaching. I then stick my nose under the building where they have their burrow set up and say, "Good morning bunnies. Is everyone okay?"

The dad bunny, whose name is Landers, replies," Good morning Merlin. It's a bit cold this morning."

Then I hear the mother bunny, whose name is Kivi, say, "Yes I think snow is just around the corner."

"Are all your babies there and accounted for? You haven't seen any snakes or any other critters trying to get in here have you?" I ask.

"Yes everyone is here and safe. No, we had a peaceful night, but did hear the coyotes carrying on earlier this morning but they never got close to us," Kivi says.

"Good, because you never know with those coyotes. You can't trust them. Do you think the babies will be coming out later today to eat and play in the grass?" I ask.

"Yes I think so, why?" Landers asks.

"Because they are teaching me how to run and jump through the air the way you all do," I reply.

"They will be out later when it warms up. I hear your guardian calling you so you better go," Landers says.

"I know she has been calling me for a while now. My guardian doesn't understand my routine so she usually has to holler for me a couple more times to come after Miracle and Rocky are already inside waiting on me. See you all later," I reply.

As I am backing my nose out from under the shed I hear everyone say, "See you later Merlin."

After breakfast it is naptime because we all know that soon we will all be going back outside while my guardian tends to the horses, the cows and the barn cat that just had kittens.

Along with the families of rabbits there is a family of raccoons. Both the rabbits and raccoons are unique in their own way. Of course the rabbits have nothing to do with the raccoons, as they are a threat to the rabbits. Raccoons eat rabbits if they can catch them so they have to be aware of them at all times. Of course I help out, if I see a raccoon coming up on the rabbits I go running as fast as I can, barking my head off to scare them away. One of the raccoon kits, whose name is Crudis, loves to tease me and make fun of me, calling me names.

While I am out playing and looking for something to chew on, Crudis starts calling me a killer, and yelling that I am a bad dog since I am a Pit Bull.

He gets his brothers and sisters to chant, "Merlin the killer Pit Bull" over and over again. Miracle and Rocky come up to me and tell me to ignore him, that he is just mean and a bully.

Miracle turns to me and says, "Don't listen to him, he's just jealous. They say the same thing about Rottweilers and look at me. Of course, that's why I ended up in that shelter, but you came and got me out, Merlin. If it wasn't for you and our guardian, they would have killed me by now. So see, you're not a killer."

I turn and look at Miracle and say, "How do you know I'm not a killer?"

"Well, have you ever killed anything?" Miracle asks.

"Yes, I have," I reply.

"Really and what exactly have you killed?" Miracle asks.

"Well once I was playing with this weird chicken that our guardian gave me to play with and I ended up chewing off its legs and wings and pulled out all of its stuffing," I reply.

"That was a toy. You can't kill a toy," giggles Miracle.

"No, you're wrong because when our guardian saw what I did she said, "Look at the mess you made and you killed the chicken," I explain.

Both Miracle and Rocky are now laughing at me so hard that they are rolling around on the ground.

Rocky says while still laughing, "Come on Merlin let's go see if we can find you another chicken to kill."

"I don't know what you two are laughing at. I really did pull its wings and legs off and pulled the stuffing out of it," I reply.

Miracle says, also still laughing, "That settles it then Merlin, you are a killer."

The three of us walk to the other side of the house where the ponds with the Koi fish are. We all look at each other and tilting his head Rocky says, "I don't hear the water running for the ponds."

I walk over to my favorite place on a rock to get a drink out of the pond and sure enough, nothing is moving. As I bend my head down to get a quick drink of water from the pond before my guardian sees me, one of the Koi swim up to where I am standing. It doesn't look good. Its color is fading and it can barely move. The other two are hiding under a rock and they don't look good either. I heard my guardian on the phone earlier talking to someone about it and that they would be here soon to take care of it, but as I am standing on the rocks looking down at the Koi, I know something needs to be done soon. I let out a bark to try and let the fish know that help is coming. I just don't know if they understand me.

While standing there, I hear a truck coming and look over toward the driveway and see a truck pulling up onto our property and realize it is the guy who had been here before working on the pond. I remember him telling my guardian to keep that Pit Bull away from him, that he doesn't like that kind of dog and is afraid of Pit Bulls. I have a feeling of darkness come over me when I look at him, which makes me feel that he can't be trusted.

He starts yelling and honking his horn so my guardian will come out and get us. He is not about to get out of his truck while the three of us are out there. Once in the house I know I can stand by the back sliding doors and keep an eye on him, as there is just something gnawing at me about this guy. As I am watching, he starts working and throwing his tools around, as the job isn't going like he was hoping. Watching this go on I feel a sense of naughtiness come over me. As I stand there staring at him, all of a sudden his tools start moving out of his reach, the water in the fountain starts spraying him, getting him all wet.

I look at what is going on and have no idea how this is happening but I am really enjoying watching his tools move around and him scrambling trying to get out of the way of the water. The water seems to follow him wherever he goes causing him to fall down a few times and then I hear him yell out in pain as he lands on his butt. While watching this in amusement, I hear my guardian laughing and yelling my name to come get a treat. She says, "I need to go check on the fountain guy. I think he hurt himself."

Oh boy, I think to myself, *I really love treats*. As soon as I turn around toward my guardian to get my treat, everything stops, the tools quit moving and the water quit spraying. I hear him yell at my guardian that he isn't able to get the fountain running, walks over, gets in his truck and just leaves. I stand there for a minute eating my treat and thinking back on what I had just seen, shake my head and go to the door so my guardian will let me out now that he is gone. I know the Koi will be in big trouble if the fountain doesn't start running again.

I run over to the pond and stand on the rocks looking down at the fish, wishing there is something I could do.

They weren't moving much and one of them looks like they are not going to last much longer under these conditions. I run to get my guardian but she is right behind me, twisting knobs and smacking pipes, anything to get it running again.

She says out loud, "I have got to get this running or these fish are going to die without oxygen and the water being filtered."

She lifts up the lid where the pump is and starts banging it. The pump is running but still no water was moving. My guardian says to herself, "One of the pipes must be frozen." I have no idea what that means and as I keep watching the fish, I feel my tail pointing in the direction of the pump. When I turn to look, the pump is pumping the water again. I think, *well that's weird, my tail starts acting up pointing in all different directions and the next thing the water is running. Did my tail have something to do with it? That's silly. How could my tail get the water running again?*

My guardian says, "I guess there was some ice that was blocking the water from running and with the sun and me beating on the pipes it must have melted enough for the water to get through or I dislodged the ice enough. Either way it doesn't matter, we got it running again, something that expert couldn't do."

Now I think to myself, *see that explains it, ice was blocking it and with my guardian banging on the pipes got the ice to move so the water would run. What was I thinking? My tail can't fix pipes.* I walk over again to the fish and they are looking better and starting to swim again. As I look down at them, one of the Koi swims over to me and winks. I have to do a double take and look down at the Koi again but they all swam off. I think, *did I just see that fish wink at me? Naw, it must have been the sun glaring off the water that made it look that way. Fish don't wink, do they?*

With that thought now gone, I start to turn around to follow my guardian back into the house. I can feel my paws starting to slip on the rocks and into the pond I fall. My guardian hears the splash and comes running. She says laughing, "How in the world did you manage to fall in? Let's get you out of there and dried off. Of course you're going to stink, so we will need to give you a bath."

A bath, I think. *I hate that kind of bath my guardian gives me. .*

As I am walking back to the house trying to shake off as much water as I can, I see Crudis off in the distance laughing at me and I feel an uneasiness swell up inside and I know something is about to happen, something bad.

Crudis yells, "How's them bunnies doing under the shed? Getting big, I bet."

Chapter Three
The Quonset

The next day, I am out playing with Rocky and Miracle in the yard, running around the trees, racing each other and playing with the rabbits. I hear Rocky and Miracle arguing about something. They are always arguing about something.

I hear Rocky say, "You know, you coming here was not my idea but they made me feel bad that you were in that place. I didn't know you were going to be such a pushy thing."

"Pushy, I'm not pushy," Miracle yells.

"Are you kidding me? You just about knock everyone over to be the first to eat, the first out the door, the first at everything. I thought I could tolerate you but again you're pushing it," Rocky shouts.

I interrupt and say, "Come on you two. Knock it off. We should be having fun not fighting. So what do you two want to do?"

"Don't ask me ask her. She always gets her way anyway," Rocky shouts.

"Okay Rocky maybe I am a little pushy so I am asking YOU, what do you want to do?" Miracle asks.

"Let's go around back and see if there is anything exciting going on," Rocky replies.

We are all in agreement and head to the back of the house and where I once again notice this half-moon metal building that sits off from the house a ways. For some reason this building always looks very familiar to me but I can't put my paw on it. I tell Rocky and Miracle that this building played a role in me being brought here but I can't quite remember. I say to them, "Let's go down and check it out and maybe that will help me remember."

As we get closer to the building, which I now know is a Quonset, off to one side a small house starts to appear. This has not happened before when we would come down here to play. We are all standing there looking at it then at each other trying to figure out where this house is coming from. As we are standing there, we start to hear voices coming from inside this house.

Miracle turns to me and says, "Merlin this is your idea. You go first and see what's inside."

I am standing there trying to muster up the courage to enter when this white Husky whom I recognize from bringing me here comes walking out of the door. I am caught by surprise seeing her.

"You, you were the one that took me from my mother and brought me here. Why did you take me away from my family?" I ask. I can feel tears starting to form in my eyes. As I stand there looking at her, I notice a large scar on her right front leg.

She walks over and licks my tears and says, "Merlin my name is Kiya and I am your elder wizard. I think you are now old enough to understand. I have been watching over you from the time you were born. We knew you were special but also in a very dangerous situation. The day I came for you I knew I had to get you out of there or it was going to be too late and you are too important to take a chance with your life."

"That scar on your leg, is that from the day you took me? Did Turbo do that? And what makes me so important?" I ask.

"Yes, Turbo tried to stop me from taking you and used his powers. Unfortunately, he got me in the leg as we were leaving. You too have magical powers, Merlin," Kiya replies.

"I don't have magical powers. What makes you think I have magical powers?" I ask.

"Every once in a while, an animal is born with a special gift. We don't know why or where it comes from, just that they have it. When you were born the Elders felt your special gift and we started watching to make sure you were going to be okay until the time came for us to get you. Unfortunately, you were born in that evil place and things were getting far too dangerous and we felt we needed to act immediately," Kiya explains.

I look at her and say, "But you left my mother, brother and sisters there."

"I thought I had more time and was going to get them out too but things happened so fast that I grabbed you and brought you here and was not able to get to the rest of your family. I'm sorry, but know that they are all still alive and you will reunite with them soon," replies Kiya.

"Why not now?" I ask.

Kiya looks at me and says, "You are not prepared for the fight you are going to face when saving them. We need to train you and prepare you so you are able to defend yourself. Your friends over there will also be trained to help you. Merlin, you can't do this alone, you need to trust me."

I turn to look back at Miracle and Rocky, who are standing there shaking their heads.

"Merlin we are both with you and want to help save your family but we need to listen to Kiya and do as she tells us to do so we can be prepared to go save them," says Miracle.

I think to myself, *Miracle is right I need to trust her but I'm going to be cautious.*

Kiya looks at the three of us and says, "Let's go inside."

Kiya goes in first, I am right behind her. I can hear Rocky and Miracle arguing about who was going next. I turn to them saying, "Will you two knock it off and come on." I can still hear them fussing at each other but Miracle finally catches up to me, then Rocky. We walk out the other side and I can't believe my eyes. It looks like I'm at the Sugar Ranch but then again I'm not. I can see our house and the barn and I can even see the horses but I can't hear them or even smell them, you know that horse smell that they have. I am not able to pick up their scent or anything for that matter. I turn and look at Rocky and Miracle and they are looking just as confused as I am.

As I stand there watching and trying to make sense of it all, there are other different types of animals running around. There are different breeds of dogs, cats, birds, and horses, but there are also some that I have never seen before. There are some that are half horse and half man, horses with wings, horses with horns in the middle of their forehead, half cat and half peacock. I can go on and on about all the different animals here. As I am standing and watching, I hear a bell ring and everyone starts heading in different areas, down hallways and through entrances that are made of trees, bushes and vines.

We walk past one area where the door is made out of heavy vines with flowers that smell really good growing on the vines. I glance in and they are all sitting there listening to and watching the animal that is standing in front of them talking. I glance over at Kiya who has a look of amusement on her face and ask, "What is this place?"

"This is Asgard. Welcome!" Kiya shouts with great pride.

Chapter Four
Asgard – Magical Training Facility

"Asgard exists in another dimensional plane where the matter is denser and more durable than the world where the Sugar Ranch is. That is why it looks like the Sugar Ranch inside the Sugar Ranch because it is," explains Kiya.

"What happens here at Asgard and why are we here?" I ask.

"You three are here because of your magical powers. Here you will have Mentors that will help you find and develop your powers," replies Kiya.

"What is a Mentor and how do you know we have magical powers?" I ask.

"Mentors are like teachers, trainers as it were. The Elders here at Asgard have the power to look out into the world that you all live in and see who has these magical gifts and who doesn't and when the time is right we come for you," replies Kiya.

"You come for us? Does that mean I will never see my guardian again?" I ask.

"Oh no Merlin, you will continue to see your guardian just as you have been. That will not change and eventually she will be brought into this magical world too, but it is not the right time for her," says Kiya.

"It sure isn't. I don't know if it's the right time for me, us, if we're even ready. But you have my curiosity going so tell me more," I reply.

Kiya continues, "Okay well, Asgard is conceived as being on earth. Just this side of heaven is a rainbow bridge which connects Asgard to heaven."

I look around and see that this place sits by the edge of the woods and in the distance is a hill and at the foot of that hill there is a lush, green meadow where time seems to stands still.

"I feel like nothing is moving forward as I look about this place," I say to Kiya.

"Time does stand still there. When an animal dies that has been especially close to their human, they go to Rainbow Bridge where they run and play in the meadows and on the hill. There is always plenty of food, water and sunshine. Any animal that is ill or old is restored to health and vigor. Those who are hurt or maimed are made whole and strong again. The animals are happy and content except for one small thing, they each miss the human whom they had to leave behind. They all run and play together, then one day one of them will suddenly stop and look into the distance as they see and feel something. So they begin to run from the group, flying over the green grass heading in the direction where they feel someone is coming for them. Their legs are carrying them faster and faster. Then the animal spots their special human and when they finally meet, they cling together in a joyous reunion, never to be parted again. Then they cross Rainbow Bridge together and enter heaven. Wild animals and others who didn't have relationships with people go straight to heaven where they will have eternal life," explains Kiya.

As Kiya is telling us about Rainbow Bridge, I can see all of that happening, dogs and cats racing over the green grass and seeing their special human and jumping into their arms. I even see horses running up to nuzzle with the human they left behind.

I am looking at Kiya and say, "My guardian said that is where Mikayla went when she left me and that she watches over me like a guardian angel. Can I go see her now?"

Kiya looks at me and says, "I'm sorry, no. You can't go see her now but one day you will meet her in those meadows and will never be apart again."

I think to myself, *I wish I could see her now, it makes me sad to know she is there and I am here.*

Kiya then says, "Let's continue. You see earth is the world of human civilization. Asgard was the home and fortress of the Aesir, one of the two tribes of the gods. Asgard was destroyed following a Secret Invasion by an enormous fiery demon native to the dimension of Asgard. This demon was affiliated with fire giants whose eyes glowed red hot with long black hair. He had superhuman strength and could cause flames to circle around him. When wounded, his blood glowed."

"I'm sorry, but did you just say an enormous fiery demon?" ask Miracle.

"That is exactly what she said," laughs Rocky.

"I don't know what an enormous fiery demon is but it doesn't sound like something I want to meet. Just where is this demon now?" asks Miracle.

"Why is the big bad Miracle scared of this demon?" asks Rocky.

"Rocky, you need to mind your manners and let Kiya answer my question," says Miracle. Rocky starts giggling.

"You don't need to worry about him. He was defeated and destroyed a long time ago," replies Kiya.

I think to myself: *thank goodness. Miracle would have driven us all crazy over that one.*

"Anyway," Kiya says. "He was possessed by evil intelligence and vast power. He unleashed his rage in fire to achieve a doomsday prophecy and under the impact, the structures of Asgard came crashing down. In an effort to consolidate and protect the power of Asgard, Asgard laid domant for thousands of years.. The ice storm came shortly after the fires. When the ice storm ended, the sun appeared and the melting began. That is when all the different animals with magical powers now known as Mentors came together and created this magical training facility for all animals. You might see a human every once in a while but know that they are very special humans and you will learn more about them in your Human Studies class."

"Come, let me show you around," says Kiya.

I am taking a quick glance around and see animals running really fast and jumping over things and running through tube like objects. Some others are changing themselves into other types of animal. There is one that really catches my attention, it is a horse-like creature that has a human head, chest and arms but otherwise looks like a horse.

I say out loud to whoever is listening, "We have horses at the Sugar Ranch but not like this."

Kiya comes over to me while I am watching this creature with such amazement.

"He is going to be one of your mentors, his name is Mentor Whinny-Huston. He is a Centaur and he teaches the Human Studies class I was telling you about," says Kiya.

I turn to Kiya and ask, "Will I learn about my guardian in this class?"

She shakes her head and says, "Yes, this is where you will not only learn about your guardian but all humans, the good ones and the bad ones."

"Let's continue with the tour and meeting some more of the Mentors who will be evaluating and teaching you how to use and control your powers," Kiya says.

"Powers? What do you mean powers? Do we all have these powers and if so how did we get them?" I ask Kiya.

"Animal magic comes in different forms, from having a sense that helps rescue a family member to finding a survivor in rubble. Some support humans with trauma and tragedies and other issues. Every animal is a spiritual teacher and guide. All animals have magic of some kind, however their powers of magic become stronger through an injury, trauma or surgery," explains Kiya, looking at me. Then she says, "Merlin, yours comes from the trauma and illness you endured by being in that puppy mill, and Miracle's comes by being in the shelter and her eye surgery.

"Rocky's, on the other hand, stems from his injury when he was hit by a car fracturing his leg as well as being given up by his human because his human couldn't afford to pay any of the medical care. Rocky desperately needed to have his fractured leg treated which ended up landing him in a shelter," explains Kiya.

I look at Kiya and say, "How do you know all that?"

"I told you, we have been watching," she replies.

As we start walking down another path towards another classroom, I hear my guardian calling all three of our names and saying it was time to come in. I look at Kiya, who is shaking her head saying, "Yes, the three of you need to run along as your guardian is requesting and we will continue this tomorrow.

You know there is much that you will need to learn in order to defend yourselves and others from the evil of humans. The evil of these humans runs deep and for some they will stop at nothing until you or whoever they have their sites on are dead." Kiya shows us back to the opening of the dog house and we walk back through it, arriving back inside the Quonset.

I say to both Miracle and Rocky, "That last statement of hers didn't make me feel all warm and cozy inside. In fact, it really scares me."

"That's why we need to pay attention and learn everything we can to protect ourselves," says Rocky.

"Maybe you two need to learn how but I already know how to protect myself," says Miracle.

"Like you would protect yourself against that demon, how?" asks Rocky.

"Come on you two, we need to get going," I shout.

Just then I look up and here comes our guardian. I certainly didn't want her to see this doghouse, so the three of us start running out toward her as fast as we can.

 She asks, "What are the three of you doing down here? Up to no good I suppose." She continues walking toward the Quonset.

Thanks to Rocky's quick thinking, he walks up to our guardian and stands in between her legs, which means, "I need a butt scratching."

Of course, our guardian knows immediately what Rocky wants and starts scratching his back and behind. After a minute or so of that and Miracle and I chasing each other, our guardian forgets all about the Quonset and says, "Hey you two, stop playing around unless you don't want dinner."

I think: *dinner of course I wanted dinner.*

We all start back to the house. As we walk toward the house, I turn around briefly toward the Quonset and the doghouse that was in the Quonset a minute ago is disappearing. I motion for the other two to look, when they do they to see the dog house slowly disappear. They both turned back to me and shrug.

Chapter Five
Meeting More Mentors

I didn't get much sleep thinking about everything that happened. I also had a terrible dream about my mother being in a terrible place. She was crying out for her puppies and also in pain and there was nothing I could do about it. I woke up very upset.

Kiya says when we return she will take us around to meet more of the Mentors. I wonder if one of those Mentors is going to show me how to find my mother and my siblings as well as save her from whatever evil is going on.

I am also excited to see what other types of creatures will be teaching us after meeting Mentor Whinny-Huston, the Centaur.

Morning comes and it is time to start our day. I think to myself: *this day will start just like every day, the three of us going outside while our guardian is preparing our breakfast. After eating breakfast, we will take a nap knowing we will be going back outside shortly to take care of everyone in the barn.*

Our Guardian comes into the room and says, "Okay, everyone wake up. I need to go to the barn for a while." The three of us jump up and head to the door. While we are standing there waiting for our guardian to open the door, I look at Miracle and Rocky, confirming we are going to be heading to the

Quonset once we get outside. Finally our guardian opens the door and out we go, running as fast as we can.

"You three be careful out here. I don't want anyone getting hurt. I have enough to take care of in the barn with those kittens," says our guardian.

Of course for some reason Miracle always has to be the first out the door. She will knock you over if you get in her way. Now the three of us are outside and our guardian is heading to the barn and we are heading to the Quonset. As we start to approach the Quonset, all of the sudden the doghouse starts to appear again. This doghouse, as it starts to appear has the look of a barn. The siding is red and the trim and roof is white. The roof extends over the opening and has a Cupola on top with a bell inside that rings when you entered the doghouse. The inside walls appear to be insulated and has wallpaper on them with pictures of different animals and the floor has very soft carpeting that feels really nice on the paws. Since the weather at the Sugar Ranch side is getting colder, you can feel warmth upon entering the doghouse. The door to enter, however seems to change size based on the size of the animal trying to enter. When you enter the doghouse from the Asgard side, it looks exactly the same. I think: *I wonder if my guardian tried to get in if it would become big enough for her to fit through.*

Then Kiya comes out of nowhere and says, "Are you three ready to meet more of the Mentors?" We are all shaking our heads and walking toward her very excitedly, following her through the doghouse and coming out the other side in Asgard.

As I look around, there are all kinds of activities going on. There are animals playing ball where this machine is tossing balls out to them and they are chasing after them. Another machine is tossing Frisbees through the air and animals are leaping as high as they can in the air to catch them. There are animals that have these weird poles with nets hanging off the poles that are sitting by a lake catching critters that have the head of a horse and the body and tail of a snake. As soon as they catch one, they set it back in the water to swim away. They are keeping track of how many each catch.

"You have already met your Human Studies Mentor, so let's move on," says Kiya.

As we're walking I stop as I see something that again looks like a horse, only this one has a golden horn coming out of its forehead. I stop and think: *Boy I have sure seen a lot of different creatures here that have horse heads with different types of bodies.*

Kiya can't help but notice me staring at him. She walks up to me and says, "He is a Unicorn and he teaches Healing and Protective powers. That is Mentor Neighberry. Unicorns are very special and rare. It is known that 'the blood of a unicorn' will keep you alive, even if you are an inch from death, but at a terrible price. You have slain something so pure and defenseless to save yourself, you will have but a half-life, a cursed life, from the moment the blood touches your lips. You will be doomed to live somewhere between life and death," explains Kiya.

I look at Kiya and ask, "Why would anyone want to kill something so beautiful?"

"Merlin," she replies, "there is great evil in the world and some humans and even other creatures are only out to benefit themselves and things like that do not matter to them as long as they benefit from it. Unicorn blood is very popular on the black market and very hard to get, which is why it costs a lot of money to purchase it. It is also illegal to sell Unicorn blood, which is why it is sold by criminals."

"What happens to them if they get caught?" I ask.

"The consequence for even getting caught with Unicorn blood is death as it is believed that you killed a Unicorn in order to get his blood," says Kiya. "Let's continue."

"I think you will find this next Mentor very interesting," says Kiya.

We walk through an opening in some bushes and there is a class that has all kinds of different animals weaving in between poles coming out of the ground then running up one side of a ladder then down the other side. There are others that are jumping over sticks that are raised off the ground and through colorful tunnels. There is an oval dirt track and when a horn sounds, whoever is on the track starts running as fast as they can to cross the finish line. There are all these obstacles that keep popping up out of nowhere that they either have to catch, jump over or run around.

"Why are they doing all of that?" Miracle asks.

"It teaches them to change their body's position quickly and efficiently. This kind of nimbleness requires balance, coordination, strength, speed, and endurance," says Kiya.

"Why would we need to be able to do all of that?" Rocky asks.

"You never know when you might be in a situation where you need to get away quickly and there may be obstacles in your way and this training will teach you how to move around them as quickly as possible to get away. These maneuvers can be lifesaving," says Kiya.

"What have we gotten into?" asks Miracle.

"Miracle, quit being such a baby," snaps Rocky.

I can see where this is going and say to both of them, "Stop. That's enough. Everything is going to be okay."

I think to myself: *I sure hope everything is going to be okay.*

At the front of the class is a big Mackerel Tabby Cat whose fur looks like it has gold and pearl fairy dust all over it. I notice right away the big "M" on her forehead.

I look at Kiya and say," I have seen many cats but never one that big."

With a slight chuckle she says, "That is Mentor Purrcotta. She is known as a Tabby Maine Coon Cat, one of the largest domesticated breeds of cat."

I then can't help but notice the strange creature standing next to her, but before I can ask, Kiya says, "And standing next to her is Skittlez; she is a cross between and monkey and cat known as a Monkat. Skittlez is a trainer to help you get on the Celestial Animalympics team. She will be working with you to help you figure out what skills you are good at and then help you fine tune them for competition at the Animalympics."

"What is the Animalympics?" I ask.

"It is where you compete against each other to determine who the best is," replies Kiya.

"Why do we need to determine that?" I ask.

"It's more for sport, like the Olympics in the human world. But it will also help you when you are battling to save your life or the lives of others. All the different maneuvers you will learn, like speed, agility, will all come in handy," says Kiya.

Rocky turns to Kiya and asks, "I hate to change the subject but does that *M* on her forehead mean anything?"

"You are very observant Rocky. Actually the *M* is the mark of a true Tabby. Some believe it to mean the breed Maine Coon, but this marking is seen on any breed of cat that has Tabby markings," explains Kiya.

"Did you see the claws on her? I bet she can tear you to shreds," I reply.

"Oh yes Merlin, and she sharpens them every chance she gets. You don't want to meet up with one of those claws," says Kiya.

I can feel Mentor Purrcotta staring at me, her eyes following me as I move. I think to myself: *I don't think she likes me. I will have to ask Miracle and Rocky what they think or if I'm just being silly.*

I realize Kiya has stopped talking while I was having those thoughts in my head. I turn to Rocky and Miracle and say, "We need to be kinder to the cats at the Sugar Ranch and not chase them up trees anymore for fun."

They both shake their heads in agreement. Mentor Purrcotta is listening to what I am saying about chasing cats up trees and says, "I might have to teach these three a lesson later about how to respect and treat cats when I have them in class. This teasing and chasing cats up trees will not be tolerated."

Kiya then notices that much time has passed and says, "It's time to get you to your first classes. You can meet the rest of the Mentors later." Kiya rushes us back out through the bushes and down the path a little further where there is a doorway in the middle of nowhere. We all three walk through the door and Kiya says, "This is where you are going learn how to move things using your minds and in some situations Merlin, by using your tail to make things move. Your Mentor for this class is a Dragon by the name of Na'vi," Kiya says, "Dragons are very intelligent and civilized creatures. Some believe they stand on the same level as humans or even higher."

I think to myself: *did she say my tail?* Thinking back to the day the pond stopped working, maybe it was my tail that made those things fly around and caused the water to spray that man and get the water flowing again in the pond.

As we enter the classroom and before Kiya can introduce me, I hear Na'vi say, "Welcome Merlin. Everyone this is Merlin and his friends Rocky and Miracle. They are just starting with us."

I continue to stare at Na'vi, as he is speaking to me and the entire class without moving his mouth or making a sound, but we can all hear him. As I look around at the other animals I hear a monkey say, "Hi Merlin glad you are here."

A horse says, "Yes and who are your friends again?"

A coyote says, "Welcome. Aren't you the one with the magic tail we have been hearing about?"

None of them are moving their mouths either.

I say to Rocky and Miracle, "A magic tail. That's news to me and did you hear that monkey, horse and coyote speak to me?"

They both shake their head no.

Miracle whispers to Rocky, "Do you think he is losing it?"

"I hear them and I am not losing it. I hear them speak without moving their mouths. Maybe with luck you two will learn how to do it," I snap.

Others are speaking to me using their mouths and actual words. I turn and look at Kiya, who is standing there with a grin on her face and before I can get the words out she says, "Yes Merlin, you have the power to do this as well as your friends and are going to be learning how."

Then I feel a nudge and turn around and Miracle is pointing to a group of coyotes laughing at us for some reason.

"What are they laughing at?" I ask.

"I think they are laughing at us," says Miracle.

"Why?" I ask.

"I don't know. You want me to go over there and ask them?" asks Miracle.

"No just leave it alone. It doesn't matter," I reply.

The one who appears to be their leader is a big coyote whose name is Romulas and who spoke to me earlier without moving his mouth. Standing behind him are four smaller coyotes.

One of the smaller coyotes, who seems to be his right hand man is called Yippy Yap and says, "So that's the Pit Bull with the magical tail that Kiya had to save that we have been hearing so much about. Doesn't look like much of a Pit Bull to me."

"I can see why she had to save him. He's a bit on the puny side for being a Pit Bull. Maybe that's why he needs that big Rottweiler next to him, to protect him. We'll see how magic that tail is when I get through with him," Romulas snarls.

I can hear them all laughing again.

"If I don't look like a Pit Bull then what do I look like? So they're laughing because Kiya saved me or because they think I'm small?" I ask.

"You look exactly like a Pit Bull and who cares what they say? They think I am your body guard so just let them think that," says Miracle.

I turn and look at Miracle who sees the fear in my eyes and says, "Don't worry Merlin, Rocky and I are not going to let that group of bullies hurt you."

Then Hazard, one of the smaller coyotes, perks up and yells, "What's the matter Merlin? Cat got your tongue?"

And just as I was about to answer back, Mentor Na'vi says, "That's enough, boys. Now sit down this minute or you will be sitting in detention." I don't know what detention is but just the word alone did not sound like a place I wanted to have to go.

"This might be something we will have to settle later," says Romulas, turning and looking at the three of us and showing his teeth.

Yippy Yap says grinning, "Yeah later!"

Chapter Six
Human Studies

Kiya arrives just as we are leaving class and says, "Your guardian is calling for you three. You better get going and we'll see you tomorrow. Can you find your way back to the dog house?"

"I think we can find it between the three of us," replies Miracle.

"Miracle, are you sure?" I ask.

"Yes we'll be fine," says Rocky.

As we are walking, I hear Miracle and Rocky arguing about which way to go.

"I have to agree with Rocky, let's try turning right," I reply.

"Really Merlin, you always side with him," snaps Miracle.

"I'm not siding with anyone. I just think this is the way to the doghouse. See, there it is. Let's run and see who gets there first," I shout.

Miracle is running as fast as she can toward the doghouse. She turns around and says, "Ha, I beat both of you." Then she turns back around and walks through the door.

I turn to see where Rocky is and I yell, "Come on Rocky lets go get dinner."

Rocky walks up to me and says, "Thanks for waiting for me, Merlin."

"Come on, let's go eat," I reply.

We walk through the door together and come out in the Quonset. Miracle is waiting for us and says, "What took you two slow pokes so long? I'm hungry."

We are walking out of the Quonset and our guardian sees us and yells, "Come on you three, it's time for dinner."

The next morning is like all mornings. We get up and go outside. The mornings are cold, I can see my breath as I take off for a run around the trees. The grass feels icy and crackles under my paws. The trees glisten with the sunlight. I run over to check on the ponds and there is a very thin layer of ice. I can see the fish swimming around. Miracle and Rocky meet up with me at the pond.

While the three of us stand looking at the pond we start talking about the class we have today: Human Studies.

"So today we will learn about our guardian. What is it that you guys think we are going to learn that we don't already know?" I ask.

"I have no idea. I think we know everything about her," Miracle says.

"Well apparently we don't, so let's go eat breakfast and get through our morning so we can go find out," replies Rocky.

"I'm just excited to learn more about Whinney Huston. I find him to be interesting, being half human and half horse. Rocky's right, let's go eat and do what we need to do inside so we can get back to Asgard," I shout.

Our guardian calls us to tell us it is time for her to go to the barn and for us to go play for a while. She opens the door and the three of us go running out and straight to the Quonset. The closer we get the more we see the dog house forming.

"I want to go first," yells Miracle.

"No I should go first, I'm older," argues Rocky.

"I don't care who goes first, let's just go," I shout.

Miracle charges through the door, Rocky is behind Miracle and I am following in last.

"We better hurry or we are going to be late for Human Studies," says Miracle.

We arrive at class just in time. Mentor Whinney Huston is trying to get everyone to settle down and be seated.

Mentor Whinney says, "In this class you are going to be learning about bad people, the people of the darkness that you are going to have to fight against to help and defend all the animals in the animal kingdom."

I think to myself: *this sounds really scary and to fight against them . . . I don't know about this.*

"You are going to learn about the good people and how out of the good people, your guardians are chosen. These are the people that will be standing next to you to help in the fight," says Mentor Whinney.

Now I am thinking: *if my guardian is there then I won't be so scared.*

"I know some of what I talk to you about you may not understand right away, but trust me, the more you know about these humans the better prepared you will be to fight," continues Mentor Whinney.

An animal sitting behind me asks, "What about money? Can we use our magic to make money so our human can buy us anything we want?"

"Money is something that cannot simply materialize out of thin air, or the economic system of the human and wizard's world would then be gravely flawed and disrupted. Guardians of magical creatures do not exploit the creature's power, when a guardian is chosen they take an oath to watch over and protect the magical creatures once the Elders feel it is time for a guardian to become part of our world," explains Mentor Whinney.

The same animal sitting behind me asks, "But what about the bad humans that have animals? "

"You are getting ahead of yourself. You first need to learn the basics so you can understand the more complicated things later," says Mentor Whinney.

This animal shouts, "Well that sounds boring. I know money is made out of paper and I like to eat paper."

Some of the other animals burst out laughing. I turn around to see who this animal is that is asking all the questions. It is a goat. I think to myself: *a goat! What is so magical about a goat? Why is there a goat here?*

"Okay class, let's get some order. You have a lot to learn in a very short time and we can't learn with this going on." Everyone turns and faces Mentor Whinney so he can continue.

"Now where were we?" Mentor Whinney asks.

"You were going to tell us about bad people," I reply.

"Thank you, Merlin. To simply put it, bad people do bad things. Bad people will try to confuse you into believing all kinds of things. The good use their money for good, whereas the bad use their money for evil. In societies throughout time and around the world, there has always been a class of humans who seek financial wealth and all the powers that are assumed to come with it. They lie, cheat and steal to get to the top. Then once at the top, they continue to do whatever is necessary in order to stay there. Yet, they do tend to lump together the good with the bad. This is an unfortunate human shortcoming," says Mentor Whinney.

"What does all this have to do with us?" asks Miracle.

The entire class spoke out loud, "Yeah, why do we care? I can hear one voice say, 'All you're doing is putting us to sleep.'" The entire class breaks out laughing.

I step in and ask, "Mentor Whinney?"

"Class let's quiet down, Merlin has a question," demands Mentor Whinney.

"Mentor Whinney, can we talk a bit about my guardian and why sometimes for no reason she just starts crying?" I ask.

"That plays a big role in how guardians are chosen. Some humans go through a terrible tragedy. How they handle that tragedy and come out on the other side determines if that human has the kind of heart it takes to be a guardian. When a human is chosen by the Elders to be a guardian of a magical creature, they must swear to an oath. We'll go over the oath later," says Mentor Whinney.

"My guardian suffered a terrible tragedy?" I ask.

"Yes, probably the worst kind of tragedy any mother could go through, her son was murdered and even though she suffered such a loss, she turned around and donated his vital organs and saved many others lives," explains Mentor Whinney.

"So is that why she cries, because she misses him?" I ask.

"Yes. Later I will show you how you can help her feel better by bringing her son to her in her dreams. We can't bring people back to life but we can have them visit in their dreams," says Mentor Whinney.

"I don't know what all that means, but I have an idea. I kinda know how she feels being taken away from my mother when I was so young. She is still alive and I'm going to find her, but in the meantime if I can make my guardian feel better, that would make me happy," I reply.

"It was that sacrifice that alerted the Mentors that she would make a wonderful guardian and protect whoever we entrust in her care," says Mentor Whinney.

"So that's how I ended up at the Sugar Ranch?" I ask.

"Yes, let me give you an example. Miracle, you were in that shelter and they were getting ready to destroy you because to everyone that came in wanting to adopt you, you showed such aggression that the people at the shelter felt you were too dangerous and eventually felt that there was no one out there that could handle you. We knew you had these magical powers and we let you have that aggression until the right person came along, but we cut it really close trying to figure out a way to get your guardian to contact the shelter," says Mentor Whinney.

"Go figure. Miracle, aggressive? Who would have thought!" giggles Rocky.

"Rocky be quiet or I'll show you some of that aggression," snaps Miracle.

"Once the Elders discovered that humans at these shelters knew each other, we used a little magic to get them to call your guardian about you. Your guardian then called the shelter where you were Miracle and told them she would be there the next day," explains Mentor Whinney.

"Oh, I remember that trip like it was yesterday," says Rocky.

"I remember that day too. I saw her in the room and was ready to show her who was boss, but then when I went into the room and she was just standing there all I could do was run over to her, jump up and put my paws on her shoulders and give her a big kiss. My Grandpapa was with her and I went over to him and rolled onto my back so he could give me a tummy rub," replies Miracle.

"Yes, the Elders were watching the entire time to make sure things went as planned and you knew this was the person you needed to be with and who would take care of you so our job was done. That was not a coincidence that Miracle came home with you guys that day. It was a plan, a plan that was cut too close for comfort but worked out," says Mentor Whinney.

"Does our guardian know we have these magical powers?" I ask.

"No, she does not know about you or your friend's powers yet. When the time comes, Kiya will meet with your guardian and tell her everything but until then, everything must remain a secret. Does everyone understand?" asks Mentor Whinney.

I say shaking my head, "Oh, I understand. I just hope I am there when this conversation takes place. It's going to be a doozy."

Just then someone shouts out, "Waah, enough with all this sentimental stuff. Let's get to some good stuff. Tell us about the bad guys and how they become bad."

"Merlin, we will get to your guardian later, how bad guys get to be bad guys," Mentor Whinney repeats.

That same one shouts, "Better make it good before we all fall asleep, like I said earlier."

"You will be able to spot bad as bad people enjoy the company of their own or shun anyone different from themselves. The greatest enemy bad people face is none other than themselves. As such, they cannot separate from and be protected from the evil that seeks their doom. For that evil is inside them, it resides close to their very core. Bad people will always come to a bad end," says Mentor Whinney.

"What about the bad people's animals? Do these bad guys have animals and are they bad to?" asks Rocky.

"Yes, a lot of them do. No, not all their animals are bad, but the bad guys train them to be bad through abuse and lack of socialization. Those that they can't turn bad end up being used as a bait dogs or they just dispose of them. Bad people don't have any respect for life in general and that is a clear reflection of how they treat their animals. Everyone should realize right now that these are some of the situations in which you will need to use your magic to protect yourselves and to save others, but we're getting way ahead of ourselves," says Mentor Whinney.

The voice from the back of the room yells, "That's what I had in mind. Tell us some good juicy stuff: the blood and guts stuff. Tell us a story about a bad person."

"You want a story about a bad guy, huh? Let me see if I have a story on the top of my head I can tell you," says Mentor Whinney.

The voice from the back of the room says, "I don't see a story on top of your head."

Everyone in the class starts laughing.

"Okay, that was very funny. Now let's quiet down and I will tell you a story. Does everyone know what a veterinarian is?" Mentor Whinney asks.

Miracle speaks up and says, "That's where my guardian takes us if we get sick or hurt. They make us better, but I don't like going there. I get afraid that my guardian won't come back for me, but she always does."

"Yes, you are right. They are doctors for animals. Miracle, trust me when I tell you, your guardian would never leave you there. She will always come and get you," Mentor Whinney explains.

"I know but it still scares me," Miracle replies.

"There is a veterinarian who took an oath to care for animals and not cause them harm. As it turns out, humans were taking their animals to her for medical care and while in her care, she was not doing what was best for the animal. She was treating them for things that they didn't have so she could charge the owners more money. She would do diagnostic testing and order medication to be given that the animal didn't need. Sometimes the medication would make the animal sicker, which made her happy since she could then order more testing and medication. She would spend her nights trying to come up with different ways to be able to charge the owners for things, just so she could make more money. She would even charge the owners a fee if they had to pay by credit card because the medical bill was too high," says Mentor Whinney.

"Finally one of her employees could no longer stand watching her abusing these animals and started videotaping her and used that to turn her in to the authorities. The prosecutor has now filed federal criminal charges against her as well as the credit card companies, so she hopefully can never harm another animal again. So now you have a person who for whatever reason knew what was going on and did nothing until one day, when what? Did she realize that what was going on was wrong or did she have a guilty conscience? Now, can anyone answer those questions and tell us why someone who went to school to learn how to care for animals would turn around and start hurting them?" Mentor Whinney asks.

"Did that veterinarian take the same oath that the guardians take and what good is the oath if they don't abide by it?" asks Rocky.

"No, it's not the same oath. The oath the veterinarians take is written by humans, and it's because this is a human full of evil and staying true to that oath doesn't mean anything. Many humans will swear under oath to tell the truth and turn around and lie. That's because there are no consequences for lying under oath, as it is up to humans to determine if they are lying or not. It's a very flawed system. That is why there is so much crime in the human world. Now when a human is chosen to be a guardian and takes the 'magical oath,' it is protected by magic so once the guardian swears to it, it cannot be broken," explains Mentor Whinney.

I think to myself: *my guardian would always protect us no matter what. I can't imagine why anyone would what to hurt us.*

"I think she did have a guilty conscience and that the veterinarian has some wires crossed in her head that made her evil. You tell that story like it's true. Did that it really happen?" asks Rocky.

"Yes, it is true and is actually taking place right now," says Mentor Whinney.

"What happened to her?" Rocky asks.

"We are waiting to find out. Her defender is trying to work a deal," Mentor Whinney says.

"Work a deal: I hope they don't. She needs to learn a lesson," snaps Rocky.

"As soon as I know something I will update you," says Mentor Whinney.

Just then from the back of the class came a loud laugh and a familiar voice saying, "No kidding, your quite the genius."

I turn around and it is that Coyote gang. I start to say something but just then Mentor Whinney says, "That is all we have time for today. You can all go to your next class."

"One of these days I'm not going to be able to control myself," says Miracle.

The head of the Coyote gang Ramulas says, "Really Rottie, and just what are you going to do about it?"

I turn and see Miracle baring her teeth and growling like I have never heard her before. The fur on the back of her neck is standing straight up. I think to myself: *I need to get over there and stop her before this turns into a blood bath*.

I walk up next to Miracle and say, "Calm down, we'll deal with them later. Let's get to our next class."

I turn and walk toward the door but Miracle is not with me. I turn back to see where Miracle is and she is still standing there baring her teeth and growling. The coyotes are standing there laughing at her.

Chapter Seven
Mentor Whootdini

We find our way to our next class, Visions and Telepathy. When we enter the area where it is being taught, there is a very large owl standing in front of everyone explaining that this class involves using all of our senses, which include our eyes, ears, our nose, sense of taste and our extrasensory perception. I know what he is talking about, except for that extrasensory perception thing, I haven't a clue. Turns out that this very large owl that is speaking is Mentor Whootdini.

I notice the colors of his feathers are illuminating. The feathers with the light shades of brown appears to be gold while the white feathers sparkle like diamonds and the black feathers are the blackest of black, yet shiny like silk. His eyes are a bright yellow and when he spreads his wings, there are eyes on each wing that are emerald green in color.

"We are going to start off with an exercise to see who can see auras," says Mentor Whootdini.

"What the heck is an aura?" Rocky asks.

"An aura is a colorful, multilayered oval energy field that surrounds all living things. These layers contain colored bands of sounds, light and vibrations. Auras can reveal information about your thoughts, feelings and dreams. The colors vary and can be light or dark shades. When reading an aura, you must take into account the shade of color in order to be precise. This is important, as it will help you identify what type of human or animal you are dealing with based on the color of their aura. For now, just remember the color you see and we will go over the meaning of the different colors later. There is a lot to learn about auras and the meaning, but for now I just want you to see if you can see the auras of some of your classmates," explains Mentor Whootdini.

"Okay Miracle, see if you can see my aura," I giggle.

"The first thing you do is focus on your friend's forehead, the third eye area. Imagine you are looking through them. You will start to notice the aura layer around the head," says Mentor Whootdini.

I think to myself: *a third eye; I don't have a third eye.*

I ask Miracle in a joking way, "Do you see my third eye?"

She doesn't answer, so I look over at her. She is standing there in a daze. I walk over and stand in front of her and ask, "Are you okay Miracle? Did my third eye scare you?"

She doesn't respond, she just stands there with eyes wide open and a blank look on her face. Now I am scared and I don't know what is happening to her. I move right beside her and she picks up her front paw and places it on my paw, but still in a daze. All of a sudden I am looking at something that is not in the classroom. I hear Mentor Whootdini off in the distance say, "Rocky, go get Kiya and hurry."

I then hear Rocky say, "Kiya, we need you back in class, something is happening to Miracle and Merlin." I now think that at least help is on the way since I don't know what is happening. I feel Kiya come over and put one of her paws on top of Miracle's and my paws. Rocky is standing in the middle of Kiya and Miracle. All but Rocky is able to see this vision at this time, or what I think is a vision.

The three of us are watching three big men: one with a lot of scruffy facial hair, tattoos, and long, stringy, dirty blond hair. I can smell the rotting food stuck in his long, dirty, beard. One of the others has multicolored hair coming from all directions and a long dirty beard. The third one has dirty red hair with a bandana wrapped around his head. When he smiles, half of his teeth are missing. He looks like he hasn't taken a bath in a month. They all have very dirty hands with dirty, long fingernails and they are all carrying big heavy chains. I don't notice the bats they also have at the time. Somehow they manage to get a scared black male Pit Bull cornered in a dark alley. As they are approaching the Pit Bull, they start swinging their chains.

The bigger man with the smelly beard is saying, "The only thing Pit Bulls are good for is fighting, being bait for the fighting dogs or something for us to use as batting practice. Now that we have you, you are about to meet your maker." All three start laughing. The Pit Bull is now cowering in the corner, shaking. The three men are now right on top of the Pit Bull and wrapping the chains around his neck. One of the other men shouts, "We are going to hang you and beat you like a piñata with these bats."

The Pit Bull cries out as the chains became tighter around his neck, cutting into his skin. I can see the blood starting to run down his neck. Now all four of his paws are coming off the ground and he is just hanging there as the chains wrap around a piece of pipe sticking out of the building. He can't even cry out, as the chains are cutting off his air. At that moment Kiya says, "I have to stop this before they kill him." With a swoop of her tail, she takes all of us to this dark alley where the three men have this Pit Bull hanging.

"I brought you three with me so you can see the evil you will be coming up against. Also, I needed Miracle to get me to the right location where this is happening. You three remain here in the shadows and pay attention," whispers Kiya.

"But we don't know anything. We won't be able to help you," I whisper.

"Don't worry, it will be alright, but you need to watch and listen closely," says Kiya.

Miracle is now out of the daze and alert to what is going on. The three of us remain hidden.

"I will go first, then we will all take turns beating this mutt. This is going to be fun and if beating him don't kill him, we'll just shoot him with this," the big one says. Just then, the big one pulls out a gun and the other two become very excited.

"So here we go," the big one shouts. He is just about to swing his bat and Kiya steps out of the shadows while we remain under cover in the darkness.

The three of us are standing very close to each other, to where we can feel each other shaking by what we are watching. I am also afraid of what is going to happen to Kiya if these monsters get her too. And if they get a hold of her, what is going to happen to us? We have no way to get back to Asgard without Kiya. I think to myself: *is this it? Am I never going to see my guardian or the Sugar Ranch again or find my mother?*

Kiya told us not to move, no matter what happens we are to stay put. I look at Miracle who whispers, "We need to do what Kiya tells us. She will let us know if she needs us." So we stand there watching from the shadows.

The man with the red hair and bandana sees Kiya first. He says to the big one, "Where did that mutt come from?" The big man turns around and now has eyes on Kiya.

Kiya looks at the three of them and says, "I'm hardly a mutt. I'm a pure-bred Husky."

I whisper to Miracle, "What is she doing, trying to get herself killed"?

Miracle looks over at me says, "You need to be quiet before you get us all killed. She knows what she is doing."

The three men stand looking at each other, then looks back at Kiya. They are confused, as they think they had just heard that Husky talk.

Kiya, looking at the three of them says, "I have power, power beyond anything you can comprehend."

The one with multicolor hair says, "A talking Husky." He then looks at the other two and asks, "Are you hearing this?"

The other two just stand there shaking their heads. "We need to capture her and take her back and breed her," he yells. "We're going to be rich. I hear Huskies are going for a pretty penny, let alone one that can talk. Maybe her babies will be able to talk too, and that's if anyone will believe us."

The three of them forget about the Pit Bull for a minute and let the chains fall from their hands. All of a sudden, there is nothing holding up the Pit Bull and he comes crashing to the ground. He lets out a whimper when he hits the ground, but not loud enough to draw attention back to him. He continues to lay there, finally able to breathe again and watching.

The three men get in a circle to try and corner Kiya.

Kiya says to the three of them, "I know exactly what you are thinking of doing but trust me that I'm never going to let that happen. I am about to do to you what you have been doing to animals for years. It's time you learn a lesson and know how it feels to be the prey. Maybe you will all get away or maybe you will end up getting caught. Either way it doesn't matter to me."

Kiya turns back to where we are out of sight and motions for us to come. The three of us step into the light, showing much confusion and fear. Kiya winks at us to let us know it was going to be okay.

Kiya turns back to the three men and says, "What was it you told that Pit Bull lying down over there, something like, "Are you ready to meet your maker?" I can see Kiya from the side and she has quite a smirk on her face.

 The red-haired man says, "Are you kidding me? Now there is another Pit Bull and a couple of Rottweilers over there. This is more than I could have hoped for. We're going to kill you three, then finish up on the one behind us and then little lady, you are all ours."

"Sorry to disappoint you, but that is not the way this is going down," says Kiya.

Kiya is starting to whip her tail around and around. The three men stand there dazed, not knowing what is going on or what is about to happen. All of a sudden, what looks like and sounds like lightening comes crashing down next to the three men. The next thing I see is the three men disappear, or so I thought. Kiya says to us, "Look," pointing down at three good-sized rats. I know it is the three men right away, because one has multicolor fur where there was once hair, one has dirty red fur with the bandana on its head, and the other one is dirty blond with that long, smelly, dirty beard.

I hear Kiya say, "Here kitty kitty, I have dinner for you." All of a sudden around ten to twelve cats appear out of nowhere. Kiya points her tail in the direction of the rats, which draws the attention of the cats. A couple of the cats get into a pouncing position, while the rest run after chasing the rats. I see one reach its paw out and bat at the one with multicolor fur but he gets up and starts running again. Now all the cats are chasing after the rats, licking their lips as they go.

The three of us are standing there amazed at what we just saw. I say to Kiya, "Are those cats really going to eat them?"

"No, but they don't know that. The cats are just going to scare them the way they have been scaring animals. Then the cats will chase them into a field," says Kiya.

"Will they stay rats forever?" I ask.

"I don't know, that is all up to them and when they learn their lessons about how to treat animals. This is why you three were brought to Asgard. You will learn how to defend yourselves and others, just the way I did here tonight. That's what all the animals at Asgard are learning, how to use their power and become very accurate at using it. Let's go get this poor boy back to Asgard. I will take him to the infirmary, where they will be able to treat him," says Kiya.

Following Kiya over to where this Pit Bull lay she says, "Get in a circle around him."

As soon as the circle is complete, Kiya again is whipping her tail around and around, then the next thing I know is we are all back at Asgard.

I was never so happy to be back at Asgard and relieved that we were all safe. I can feel myself relaxing from all the shaking I was doing and think to myself: *I hope the next time this happens, I'm better prepared to handle it. Maybe it's my tail that will save us.*

Chapter Eight
Celestial Animalympics

"You three need to get to your next class and don't speak about what just happened to anyone. The last thing we need is to stir things up with the students and then they go out thinking they can save the world," says Kiya.

"What class are we supposed to go to?" I ask.

"You need to get to Celestial Animalympics Training. Mentor Purrcotta will be waiting. If you have any problems tell her to see me. Now do you remember how to get there?" Kiya asks.

"I think so," I say, while turning and looking at both Rocky and Miracle, who are shaking their heads.

Kiya turns and walks off with the injured black Pit Bull and we go in the opposite direction. We find the opening in the bushes and go in and just like Kiya said, Mentor Purrcotta is waiting for us.

"Where have you three been? You're late," shouts Mentor Purrcotta.

"We were with Kiya," says Miracle, before I had a chance to say anything.

"I will take this up with Kiya later. Now you three need to get over there with Skittlez so she can see what you can do, if anything, in order to compete," says Mentor Purrcotta.

"Compete for what?" I ask.

"Not compete for what, compete in. We need to see if you have any skills in running, jumping, and catching, for example, for the Celestial Animalympics," says Mentor Purrcotta.

"What does that have to do with learning what our powers are as well as how to use them flawlessly and on point in case of danger?" I ask.

"This will show us your weaknesses and strengths as well as your sportsmanship. This will determine if you will panic or remain level headed and be able to work through a situation. We can then help you with your weaknesses and improve on your strengths so you will be able to fall back on these teachings when you are in a difficult situation and know what to do. Plus, to qualify to participate in the Celestial Animalympics is like a badge of honor: the best students going up against the best," says Mentor Purrcotta.

"I have just a few more questions," I reply.

"Merlin, those are going to have to wait. I really don't have time for all your questions right now. As you go to your different classes you will not only find out what your powers are but see what powers others have," Mentor Purrcotta says. She turns and walks away before I can get another question out.

"I guess that is all you get from her right now Merlin," says Rocky.

The three of us walk over to where Skittlez is waiting.

"There is one thing that Mentor Purrcotta does not tolerate and that's tardiness. Unless you want to get on her bad side, you have to be on time. Now let's see what each of you got. Let's start with you, the Rottweiler," says Skittlez.

I think to myself: *I think we are already on her bad side.*

Miracle looks at Skittles and says, "My name is Miracle. What do you want me to do?"

Skittlez points to the track and says, "First let's see how fast each of you can run and we will go from there. Now watch for things that will magically appear and you will either need to jump over them, run around them or there might be things flying through the air that you need to catch."

Miracle walks over to the track. Skittlez says, "Now when you hear the horn, take off running as fast as you can from that line." Miracle looks over at me and grins.

The horn sounds and Miracle takes off running. I have never seen her run that fast before. All of a sudden, a fence appears right in front of her and she jumps over it. Next, a ball comes flying through the air, she leaps up and catches it in her mouth. When she lands, she drops the ball on the ground, next these tall trees appear scattered about and Miracle is zigging and zagging around them. Skittlez is standing there with a watch timing her. When Miracle comes back around and crosses the finish line Skittlez says, "That was amazing. You have the fastest time yet. You keep this up you will break some long-standing records in the Celestial Animalympics," and writes on her pad. When she finishes writing she puts the pad and watch down and turns to look at me.

"Let's see how fast you can run, Merlin. We need to get your time down and as for Rocky, I will time him after you," says Skittlez. She motions for me to get on the track and get ready.

"When you hear the horn, take off running as fast as you can until you cross the finish line," says Skittlez. She picks her watch and pad back up, she then gets the horn and pushes the button, the horn sounds.

I am running as fast as I can. I hear both Miracle and Rocky yelling, "Run Merlin, run!"

I see the fence appear and leap over it like the rabbits have taught me, then the ball. I think: *I don't want that thing in my mouth.* So I let it go, then the trees appear and I start to show off and do figure eights around them before I see the finish line coming up and start to run even faster. I look over at Skittlez and she is writing on her pad.

"How did I do? Did I do okay?" I ask Skittlez.

"Let's get Rocky's time and then we will go over everyone's results at once." Skittlez looks at Rocky and says, "You're up, let's see what you got."

Rocky is looking at me worried because since his injury, he has not been able to run very fast or for very long.

Skittlez says, "The same for you. When you hear the horn, take off running as fast as you can."

Skittles sounds the horn and Rocky starts running. He only gets a short distance when the fence appears in front of him and I see him slowing down as he approaches it. I yell, "Go Rocky," and I barely get the words out when all of a sudden his ears turn into what looks like bat wings, and instead of running he is flying and using his tail as a rudder to fly over the fence and to zigzag around the trees. Since he is already up in the air he is able to fly up to catch the ball, only he hangs onto it. He is using his tail to go around corners and change direction. I turn to look at Skittlez, whose mouth is now wide open and she drops the watch and her pad.

Skittlez turns to me and says, "Did you know he could do that? We have a lot of flying animals here but a flying dog is the first for me and to be that fast . . . amazing!"

"No, I had no idea. We always teased him about his ears but he never did that before," I reply.

Just then Rocky comes flying over the finish line and lands. I look at Rocky and he has a surprised look on his face too.

"What was that about? I didn't know you could do that and I think you can drop the ball now," I say to Rocky.

Rocky says, after letting the ball fall from his mouth, "I didn't know I could do that either. I just started running and started feeling scared that I wasn't going to make it and the next thing I knew my ears took over and I was able to use my tail to go where I wanted to go."

I look over at Skittlez and ask, "Well, did he qualify? Was he fast enough?"

Skittlez says while standing there scratching her head, "I don't know. I have never seen anything like it. I dropped my watch so I don't know how fast he was going. So flying is at least one of his magical skills."

"Well to me he looked like he was going pretty fast," I reply.

"Merlin, that's not the point. We have never had a flying dog in this particular competition. They have all been runners and jumpers. I don't know if this competition allows flying dogs. In all my years as a trainer, I never had a flying dog. I don't know why they wouldn't allow him to take part in it, though. He did complete everything and get through all the obstacles," says Skittlez.

I think to myself: I *wish one of my magical powers was to read her mind. I would love to know what she is thinking.*

"What are you going to do then? I don't want Rocky disqualified because he can't run but he can fly," I reply.

I turn to Mentor Purrcotta and say, "He's a little wobbly with his flying and turns but just needs to practice. So what do you think? Does he qualify to be on the team to compete in the Celestial Animalympics?"

55

Chapter Nine
Telekinesis – Making Things Move

Kiya got wind of what happened at the track and came looking for us. She caught up to us still standing around the track. As she walks up she sees the look on Mentor Purrcotta's face. Skittlez is standing next to her.

"Why don't you take Mentor Purrcotta back to her room and we will sort this all out later," Kiya says to Skittlez. She then turns to the three of us and says, "You need to get to your next class."

At the same time the three of us say, "Okay we're going."

We turn to leave and I see something out of the corner of my eye. It is moving very gracefully and has something that looks like it has a crown on its head and very long tail of feathers that are dragging the ground. It is the prettiest maroon color.

I turn to Miracle and Rocky and say, "Do you see that over there?"

Turning back around in the direction where I saw it.

Miracle turns and says, "See what?"

"Never mind it's gone," I reply.

"What was it?" Rocky asks.

"I have no idea. Hopefully I will see it again. It was beautiful," I mumble.

Miracle and Rocky look at each other and shake their heads as we walk down the path looking for the doorway in the middle of nowhere. We find it and walk in. The other animals that are in that class are following us in. I can hear the Coyote gang behind us laughing and carrying on. One of them yells, "Look, it's the flying mixed breed."

"Hurry up. We need to get in here and get seated before those coyotes get in here and try to start trouble," I say to Rocky and Miracle.

"Let them try. I'll make him bleed even more next time," says Miracle.

"No Miracle, Merlin's right. We don't need any trouble right now, we've had enough excitement for today. Hopefully, this is the last class we have with those coyotes for the day so let us get through it without any drama, can we?" Rocky asks.

"You're right, Rocky. So we should probably sit up front where it will be less likely for anyone to start any kind of trouble with us," says Miracle.

We find an area up front where the three of us can sit together. Just as we are sitting down, Mentor Na'vi walks in and asks, "Are we all ready to begin and learn how to make things move without touching them?" Again he is not moving his mouth.

I am very excited to start learning how to do this. I want to be able to talk without moving my mouth and to make things move. I think it is cool. I am hoping that this is one of my magical powers.

"I want you to break off into threes," Mentor Na'vi says. Of course, it is going to be Miracle, Rocky and me in a group. I can hear two of the coyotes complaining because they have to go to another group. Knowing that, I feel a smirk come across my face.

Mentor Na'vi walks around and puts a large feather in the middle of our group and says, "We are going to start off with something light to move. Now does each group have a feather?" he asks.

Everyone nods. "In order to do this, there are several things you must do. You must be relaxed. One way of doing this is by meditation to clear your mind. Then you must believe it's true. False beliefs are a well-known obstacle to achieving anything. Then you need to visualize. You will have to practice, practice, practice and be patient. You will improve your concentration every day by doing this."

He goes on to say, "Once you have mastered the feather, you will move on to a tennis ball."

I look over at Miracle whose ears pop up when she hears tennis ball. I whisper, "You won't be able to chase it, you will have to move it." A look of disappointment comes over her face.

"I want you to each take a turn and concentrate on the feather for about ten minutes until you feel like it is a part of you. Then I want you to visualize the change you want to do to the object, whether it's bending it or moving it," says Mentor Na'vi.

"I'll go first," Miracle says. Closing her eyes for a few minutes, she starts to slowly open them and looks at the feather lying on the ground. Rocky and I are both watching the feather to see if it moves. Nothing is happening after five minutes or so.

"I'll go now," says Rocky. I am watching him and he starts to close his eyes, then he slowly opens them and as he opens them he raises his front right paw and points it at the feather and it starts to move.

I say excitedly, "You're moving it." Suddenly it stops moving and I look at Rocky who says, "I lost my concentration."

"That's alright, you moved it. Now my turn," I reply. I close my eyes and clear my head of all thoughts, and then I slowly open my eyes. I focus on the feather with my eyes wide open and stare at the feather lying on the ground, it starts to shake a little bit. I continue staring at it. I hear Miracle say, "Look he's doing it." I continue to stare at the feather and then it lifts off the ground, no longer just shaking. It is flying around the room. I have no control over it. I am no longer concentrating on the feather, I am just watching it zoom around the room. Now I can't see it anymore and then hear a loud yelp. That yelp came from the coyote Romulas. I look in the direction of Romulas who is look- ing at me with a very angry face. Now I see the feather sticking out of Romu- las's behind.

"Well that explains where my feather went," I giggle. The entire class is laughing.

"I didn't mean for that to happen. It just took off on its own," I explain.

"Sure it did, little Pit Bull. You are going to pay for this," says Romulas. He turns to Yippy Yap and says, "Stop laughing and pull that feather out of me."

Yippy Yap grabs hold of the feather with his mouth and gives a yank and the feather comes out, but not without causing a little pain as Romulas whimpers.

The class continues to laugh.

"Clearly this was an accident, everyone just needs to practice more. No need to get your feathers ruffled," Mentor Na'vi chuckles.

The class is laughing hysterically now.

"That's all the time we have for today, now please bring me your feathers," says Mentor Na'vi.

"Merlin, how and why did you do that?" Miracle asks. "That was brilliant."

"I have no idea. One minute I am staring at the feather thinking nothing is going to happen, then it starts shaking and then, well you saw it, it was flying around. I had no control over it," I explain.

"That's too bad because I was going to tell you, great aim," Miracle says, laughing.

A couple of the coyotes decide to bring their feather to Mentor Na'vi by walking past me. One of them gets close enough to me and pushes me causing me to stumble into Miracle. As they continue on they are laughing and muttering something I can't understand. I can feel the anger coming off of Miracle and look up and see her snarling and snorting. I know this isn't going to end well, so before she can do anything I say, "Miracle, it's okay. We don't want to cause any trouble in here. We will take care of this later."

"Okay, but trust me, this is not over by any means," Miracle says.

Chapter Ten
Learning Healing and Protective Powers

Finally Miracle looks at me and says, "Did you say something, Merlin?"

"Yes Miracle, we need to get to our next class, we don't have time for this," I reply.

"No we need to teach these coyotes a lesson and some manners," says Miracle.

"And you think you are the one that is going to teach us?" Romulas asks.

"Why yes I do and now is the perfect time," says Miracle.

As Miracle is saying these words, she is charging the coyotes. Out of nowhere Kiya appears and grabs Miracle by the scruff of her neck. Miracle lets out a whimper. The look on Kiya's face let us all know she is not happy with what was about to happen.

"I don't know what I just walked in on, but now is not the time to take care of it." She looks at the three of us and says with eyebrows raised and eyes wide open, "I will speak to each one of you later, now get to class."

We get to our class just as Mentor Neighberry is calling out everyone's name. He turns to us and says, "I'm glad the three of you could find time to join us."

I can feel Miracle wanting to say something back so I nudge her in the side with my paw and whisper, "Not now. Let's just take a seat."

"In this class, you will learn how to use your powers to heal and protect other animals that are either hurt, in danger or both. Let me demonstrate," Mentor Neighberry says.

As he turns, I can see a bird lying on a table trying to get up but one of his wings is not working. Mentor Neighberry walks over to the bird and as he does, he lowers his head and I notice that his eyes are almost closed. Standing over the bird, he touches the golden horn on his forehead to the wing of the bird. There is a bright yellow light surrounding the bird for a minute. Once the light is gone, the bird sits up, moves both of its wings and takes off flying. I hears the whole room react with "ahh" and "ooh."

"Mentor Neighberry, how can I do something like that? I don't have a horn in the middle of my forehead. In fact none of us do," I remark.

"Yes, you're right, but you have other ways of using your powers. For example Merlin, it's your tail," Mentor Neighberry replies.

"My tail? Like the way Rocky can use his tail to steer him when he's flying?" I ask.

"Something like that," says Mentor Neighberry.

"Mentor Neighberry, my guardian has a cow that is getting ready to have a baby. Can we see her from here and see if anything is happening? I know my guardian is very worried about her, it's her first one," I ask.

"Yes, let's come over to this window," says Mentor Neighberry.

I didn't see a window, but as I stand next to Mentor Neighberry I can see my Sugar Ranch and the cows in the pasture.

Someone in the class yells, "Look, look at that cow over there. It looks like something is happening with her. She doesn't look good."

Now I see the cow my guardian calls Chrissy and she looks like she is struggling. I am looking around for my guardian but she is nowhere.

"Mentor Neighberry do you think she is okay?" I ask.

"I don't know, but let's stand here and watch her for a minute," says Mentor Neighberry.

"I sure don't like the looks of her right now," I reply.

"She is getting ready to have a baby. Now I would like everyone to come over and watch something amazing that is about to happen," says Mentor Neighberry.

The entire class is standing around watching. I shout, "Oh look what is that coming out?"

"That is the calf's front hooves. We should be seeing the head any minute now. See, here comes the head," explains Mentor Neighberry.

"That baby is quite a ways off the ground. Is it going to get hurt if it falls or is Chrissy going to lay down for the rest?" I ask.

"I don't know, let us watch and see what happens," replies Mentor Neighberry.

It happens so quickly that now the baby is lying in the snow on top of the ice. It is struggling trying to stand up and Chrissy is also trying to help the calf up but it keeps slipping on the ice and falling back down. I look at Chrissy and I see panic on her face.

"Mentor Neighberry, I think the baby is in trouble. We need to do something before it dies," I shout.

"We will give it another minute and if it can't get up, Merlin I will help you to help the calf," Mentor Neighberry says.

"Me help the calf? I don't know how to do that, you do," I reply.

"I will be right next to you and if something goes wrong I will step in," replies Mentor Neighberry.

I can hear the class saying, "Stand up baby and get with your mother." I am watching and the calf is continuing to slip on the ice and fall back down.

"Merlin, come here. We need to step in and help this calf now. He's not able to do it on his own," Mentor Neighberry says.

I am now standing right next to Mentor Neighberry and he says, "Go into your playful bow and once you do that, raise your tail up over your back and aim it toward the calf." I go into my playful bow and raise my tail up.

"Is this really going to work?" I ask.

Now everyone is standing around watching me. I say to myself: *this is crazy, what can my tail do?*

"Now what and will my power be able to go through Asgard that way to reach the calf?' I ask.

"Your power can go anywhere once you learn how to do that," replies Mentor Neighberry.

"Look, there is a green light coming out of the end of Merlin's tail," shouts Miracle.

"There is a what?" I ask.

"Quiet everyone. Now just aim that green light toward the calf and concentrate on helping the calf stand and walk to its mother," Mentor Neighberry explains.

"Look, he's doing it. The calf is standing," Rocky shouts.

"I don't know how much longer I can do this. Oh no," I shriek. The calf falls to the ground.

"Try again and concentrate," says Mentor Neighberry.

I go in my playful bow position and raise my tail up over my back. The green light is shining from the tip of my tail. I aim it at the calf and with everything I have, I try to help the calf stand.

"There you go Merlin. You're doing it but I can see you are getting tired so let me help," says Mentor Neighberry.

Mentor Neighberry, still standing next to me, lowers his head. A yellow golden light is coming from the tip of his horn toward the calf. Together we help the calf stand and walk over to its mother where she welcomes him and pushes him to where he can start to drink her milk.

"Good job Merlin," says Mentor Neighberry.

"For what? I didn't do it you did," I reply.

"This was your first try, you just needed some help. Now it looks cold out there and the calf is wet and laid in the cold icy snow for a long time. I don't think he is out of the woods yet. Let me put a protective bubble around him to help dry him and keep him warm until your guardian finds them and she can get them into the barn," whinnies Mentor Neighberry.

Mentor Neighberry turns and again points his golden horn toward Chrissy and her calf. A golden light starts shining toward them and the light starts spinning around in a circle, encompassing both Chrissy and the calf.

"That should help. Does anyone have any questions? I wasn't quite prepared to show you all that but to see it in an emergency situation was a good lesson and teaches you that a situation can happen without warning," explains Mentor Neighberry.

Now everyone in the classroom wants to save something.

"No more saving anything today. I was going to have you all practice on things that are not alive, like torn toys but we have run out of time so I will have you practice on the toys next time. Please do not practice this outside this classroom, a human might see you, placing you in danger," says Mentor Neighberry.

"How?" I ask.

"You will be learning more about the evil within humans in your Human Studies class and should one such evil human see you use your powers, well you can't even imagine what one of those evil humans would do to get their hands on you. They will try to capture you, take advantage of your power, and possibly use force to make you do the things that they ask you to do and if you don't, they just might hurt you to try and get you to change your mind," whinnies Mentor Neighberry.

That sends a chill up my spine!

Chapter Eleven

Back to the Track

I look at Miracle and Rocky and say, "Let's ask if we can go hang out at the track for a little while and practice running, since we have some time to kill."

"I would really like to try that jumping off the ramp into the water if they will let me," says Miracle.

"I think I will just sit and watch you guys," Rocky says.

"No Rocky, you are going to run the track again and practice that thing with your ears and tail. Maybe we can find Skittlez and see if you qualified to be on the team. If fact, we need to find out if any of us qualified. I want us all to be a part of the Celestial Aniamlympics, we're a team. Maybe we won't qualify but at least we tried. There are so many different things to try out for. I know there are things that each one of us are going to be great at," I reply.

"I was afraid you were going to say that. What if I can't do it again?" Rocky asks.

"There is only one way to find out and that's for you to go try. Okay here we are. What should we do first?" I ask.

We walk in and I have to look at both Miracle and Rocky to see the expressions on their faces, as there are animals here that I have never seen before. There are creatures with man bodies and dog legs, there are part cat and part peacock creatures.

I ask Miracle, "Are all these animals going to try out to take part in Celestial Animalympics?"

A voice coming from behind me says, "Why do you have something against us?"

I turn around and standing in front of me is that maroon creature, that's part cat and part peacock that I saw at the track earlier. "No but I have never seen an animal quite like you or that dog, I mean man creature standing next to you," I reply.

She replies with a giggle, "I'm sure you haven't. I am known as a Peacat. My name is Illusion. My friend here is an Adlet and his name is Maagmen."

I think to myself: *Illusion is really pretty. I wonder if she finds me handsome.*

Miracle is now poking me saying, "Merlin are you okay? What's with the goofy look on your face?

"I think Merlin's in love," Rocky replies.

I hear both Rocky and Miracle laughing and say, "I'm not in love, I just think she's pretty."

Now I hear Illusion laughing and say, "Did I just say that out loud?" Rocky and Miracle are both shaking their heads yes and laughing.

"Well it's been nice meeting you both, but we're here to practice on the track. I hope we see each other again sometime," I say.

"I hope so too, Merlin," Illusion responds.

"Come on Rocky and Miracle, let's head on over to the track," I suggest. I hear Illusion say, "Bye Merlin."

I think to myself: *don't turn around just keep walking.* I hear Miracle and Rocky giggling.

"I can hear Romulas now, if he ever sees the two of you together," says Miracle.

"What do you think he is going to say?" I ask.

"I think he is going to think you two are sweethearts and give you a really hard time about it," Miracle says.

"Sweethearts! We just met. Give me a break. Hopefully he is not that stupid," I shriek.

"I think you are giving him way too much credit and I do think he is that stupid," Miracle shouts.

"Can we just drop this whole thing and get back to doing what it is that we came here to do and that's practice?" I ask.

"Sure, if that will make you feel better," says Miracle.

"Okay." I blurt. "Rocky, you go first and let's see if those ears of yours kick in."

"I'll try," Rocky murmurs.

Rocky walks out on the track and I says, "When I yell, go Rocky, you start running."

Rocky shakes his head. I yell, "On your mark, get set, and GO."

Rocky starts running and all of a sudden his ears start looking like bat wings again and they start flapping, his paws are no longer on the ground and his tail is moving in the direction of the turns he needs to make. Now I feel something next to me and turn to look. A large hawk is standing with us, watching Rocky.

"I heard about a flying dog and had to come see for myself. He clearly doesn't quite know what he is doing, bobbing around like that. I think I can help him," the Hawk shrieks.

"And you are? I ask.

"I'm sorry, let me introduce myself. I'm Mentor Screech. Actually my name is Skessewk but that is just too hard to say if you're not a hawk so everyone just calls me Screech. I teach Flying and Teleportation. That's quite a gift your friend has there," the Hawk says.

"He didn't even know he could do that until recently when he was trying out for the team. I'm Merlin."

"Yes the Pit Bull Wizard with the magic tail," says Mentor Screech.

"Well, that's what my guardian calls me but how do you know that and about my tail? I myself am just learning about my tail and how to use it," I reply.

"You are very special and we have been hearing about a Pit Bull Wizard for some time now, but I am very glad to meet you and your friends," says Mentor Screech.

"I'm Miracle the Rottweiler," Miracle announces.

"Well Miracle the Rottweiler, it's a pleasure to meet you as well," Mentor Screech replies.

We continue watching Rocky as he comes around the last turn and overshoots it a bit but gets back on course and flies across the finish line.

"Rocky, please join us," Mentor Screech yells.

"Rocky, this is Mentor Screech. He teaches flying and something else," I announce.

"Teleportation," says Mentor Screech.

"He thinks he can help you fly better," I remark.

"What's wrong with the way I fly?" Rocky asks. "I think I do pretty well since I only just found out that I can fly."

"You're right Rocky, you do quite well, but I can show you how to make your turns sharper, how to go higher and faster," Mentor Screech replies.

"I don't think I want to go any higher or faster," Rocky replies.

Now I see Mentor Purrcotta and Skittlez approaching us.

"Mentor Screech, so what do you think? Can you train him?" Mentor Purrcotta asks.

"Yes, he has a lot of potential," Mentor Screech replies.

"A lot of potential for what?" I ask.

"For joining his team in the flying and tracking division. We are still looking into if flying dogs are allowed to compete in track," Mentor Purrcotta says.

"In the meantime, Rocky stop by my area and I can explain to you what it is we do and maybe you will want to start working with me to improve your flying," Mentor Screech suggests.

"Can Merlin come with me?" Rocky asks.

"What about me? Don't you want me to come?" Miracle asks.

"If you want to. I just didn't think you would be interested," replies Rocky.

"Of course I want to see and be there when you screw up," giggles Miracle.

"If that's the only reason you want to come, forget it. I don't need your sarcasm," snaps Rocky

"I'm kidding, Rocky. Don't get so upset. I want to be there to support you," Miracle explains, rolling her eyes.

"I will make sure she behaves herself. We need to go. I hear our guardian calling us," I announce.

"So I will see you tomorrow, Rocky?" Mentor Screech asks.

"Yes we will all be there," Rocky replies.

"Good. I will have one of my assistants meet you and bring you to my class," Mentor Screech responds.

"Okay, we need to get going. Our guardian is starting to panic," I announce.

As we turn to leave I hear a voice that I really didn't want to hear and that was the voice of Romulas the coyote.

"So we not only have a Pit Bull with a magic tail, we have a flying mix breed. And what about you blockhead, what do you do?" Romulas asks.

"I certainly hope you are not talking to me," Miracle replies.

"I don't see any other blockhead in the area, do you?" Romulas asks looking around.

I am now thinking to myself: *here we go again.*

I now hear Miracle snarling and look to see that she is crouched and baring her teeth.

"I know what you're thinking, Merlin. Don't try to stop this. This is long overdue. This coyote needs to be taught a lesson," shouts Miracle.

"But Miracle, our GUARDIAN!" I yell.

"You better worry about your guardian, she'll be next," giggles Romulas.

Chapter Twelve
Ms. Damballa LaVey

I don't know where she came from but Kiya is standing right in the middle of Miracle and Romulas.

"You three head to the Quonset and meet your guardian. As for you, Romulas, come with me. This nonsense has to stop," Kiya shouts.

"It's not nonsense. I just need to show them who is in charge around here and they need to respect that," argues Romulas.

Kiya says with a slight giggle, "I have no idea where you got the idea that you are in charge but you are far from it. Now go."

I turn to see what is going on and Kiya has Romulas by an ear marching him toward her area. I can't help but let out a laugh.

"I heard that, little Pit Bull," Romulas yells.

"And what are you going to do about it Romulas?" Kiya asks.

"I'm, I'm…" Romulas stutters.

"You're what? You're not going to do anything, now march," snaps Kiya.

"There's the Quonset. Let's go and find our guardian," I shout.

I hear our guardian say, "Where have you three been and what have you been up to? I have been searching for you. I thought I checked in here earlier and you weren't here."

Oh boy, I think, *how are we going to get out of this? How long are we going to be able to keep this quiet?*

Kiya needs to sit down with our guardian soon and explain everything and in the meantime we need to be careful that she doesn't find out on her own I say to myself.

Miracle starts barking at Rocky and Rocky barks back at Miracle and our guardian shrieks, "That's enough. Get up to the house for dinner."

We are walking up to the house and out of nowhere there is Crudis. He looks at me with a smirk and starts running toward the shed where the bunnies live. He slows down when he is close to the shed. He looks over at me again and rubs his front paws together, then licks his lips. I start barking. Miracle and Rocky start barking too and that gets the attention of our guardian. She walks over and sees Crudis very close to the shed. She is surprised and yells, "No, no you get away from there. Where did you come from? You need to go back to wherever it is you came from. There is nothing here for you."

She is clapping her hands together, making a terrible noise and yelling. This scares Crudis and he runs back toward the barn and onto the neighbor's property behind us and disappears. If I hadn't known our guardian, she would have scared me with all that noise and running around. Our guardian shouts out loud, "I wonder where he came from. I haven't seen raccoons around here in a while. Guess I need to keep an eye out for them now that I know they are back."

Back in the house, our guardian turns on the TV and there was a show on about a vet and he's operating on a dog. She changes the channel and there is a story about a shelter taking in Pit Bulls because of a new law discriminating against them. This catches my attention. They are now talking to a heavy-set woman who appears to be running this shelter. My guardian sits next to me to watch. My guardian is shaking her head and says, "Ignorant people like that make me sick. They go off half-cocked and have no idea what they are talking about. A law discriminating against Pit Bulls, what next? Don't these people have anything better to do? I am so glad we live out here in the country and there are no such laws out here."

As the woman on TV continues to speak I get a sense that she is not telling the truth. My guardian says, "I don't like the looks of her. And what, do they purposely find the dumbest person they can to put on TV and talk about it? There is something about her that I just don't trust."

I continue to sit and stare at her, thinking the same thing. Next they show the back of the shelter where all the dogs are in cages. I don't like seeing things like that, so I go in the kitchen and wait for my guardian to finish fixing our dinner. We all clean our bowls. Miracle always comes and checks my bowl to see if I left anything, I didn't.

Finally my guardian turns the channel on the TV and there are a bunch of women fighting and yelling that one of the men accused one of the women of flirting with one of the other men, whatever all that means. I think to myself: *this is the perfect time to go to sleep.*

I now hear my guardian say, "It's time for breakfast."

I didn't realize I had been asleep that long. I am kind of stiff, so as I walk to go outside before going to breakfast I have to stretch my legs. Outside I do a little stretch of my back legs then start to walk around until I find the perfect spot to go to the bathroom. I feel like I want to get in a quick run before breakfast so I take off running around the trees. The bunnies under the shed stuck their heads out and yell good morning to me. Now I hear my guardian hollering for the three of us to come in for breakfast. Once breakfast is done, the three of us are just laying around chewing on bones until it is time to go out again.

My guardian says, " We need to go take care of the horses, cows and the barn kitty a little early today, so we best get going."

I think to myself: *no, you have to go take care of all that. We have to go play and head back to Asgard. Maybe even practice with our magical powers or find out if we have more than one.*

My guardian heads to the barn and the three of us are running to the Quonset. Just as Screech promised, he has one of his assistants waiting for us. It is Illusion. I can feel a smile starting to come over my face and try to hide it, but not before Miracle sees it.

"Are you kidding me? You look like you're in love," giggles Miracle.

"Don't be silly. I just met her, but you have to admit she sure is pretty," I sigh.

"Yah, if you like a half-cat, half-peacock sort of thing," giggles Miracle.

"Leave Merlin alone, Miracle. I think it's cute and besides, I think you might be jealous," Rocky smirks.

"Cute? Don't be stupid," Miracle snaps.

"Who are you calling stupid?" asks Rocky.

"The two of you need to knock it off and let's go see what Mentor Screech is going to do with Rocky," I suggest.

"Watch him crash," Miracle replies.

I turn just in time to see Rocky stick his tongue out at Miracle and giggle.

"Yesterday when we met, your feathers where a maroon color and today they're yellow, why?" I ask Illusion.

"Oh you noticed," giggles Illusion.

"How does that happen? Is that your magic?" I ask.

"Not really. My feathers change color based on the mood I'm in. When I raise my train, I am able to hypnotize people, some animals, whatever I want. That's some of my magic. Want to see?" Illusion asks.

"Sure," shouts Rocky.

Illusion starts purring and shaking her tail, she calls it a train and the feathers come up like a fan behind her. The feathers are marked with eyespots.

"Why are there eyes on your feathers?" I ask.

"Those are the eyes of the stars. Because of that, my feathers represent immortality, and can absorb negative energies, protecting those who wear them. Now for the hypnotist part," says Illusion.

She is looking at Miracle and says, "Here we go."

"No, not me," yells Miracle.

Illusion laughingly says, "Here we are. Mentor Screech will be with you in just a minute. Take a seat. Oh and Merlin, I will see you later." I hadn't even realized that we had been walking the entire time.

I can feel my face heating up as I watch her leave. We sit down waiting for Mentor Screech to arrive and Rocky says, "Merlin, look at Miracle. I think it's happening again."

I look over at Miracle and know she is having another vision. I think to myself: *please don't let it be anything like that last vision that landed us in that dark alley.*

I place my paw down on top of her paw right as I hear Mentor Screech say, "What on earth is going on here?"

I hear Rocky say, "Miracle is." Then I don't hear anything else for a second.

Now I am seeing a sign that says:

Marion's
Gentle Animal Shelter

I am getting the feeling that this is not a gentle animal shelter like the sign says. It feels dark, like death. I hear this high-pitched squeaky voice coming from inside the building that sounds familiar. Miracle's vision now takes us inside. I can now see where this squeaky voice is coming from. There stood a woman who is very short and round. She has shoulder-length yellow hair but where her hair comes out of her head, it is mousy brown. She has big, puffy cheeks, and squinty eyes and when she walks, her thighs rub together making a cricket sound. It is that women who was on TV that my guardian said she doesn't trust and neither do I.

She is talking to a tall, skinny girl with long greasy, kinky, brown hair with streaks of yellow throughout. She has red bumps all over her face and wears glasses that make her eyes look really big. I also notice there is a fog that surrounds her, and when she talks it is a whine. This very round lady is talking to her about the fog surrounding her, calling it a stench.

The round lady says in her high squeaky voice, "Fern, how many times have I told you not to wear that rancid-smelling stuff to work. When your smell is mixed with the smell of these foul animals, it gives me a headache."

Fern says in a very whiny voice, "I'm sorry Ms. Damballa. Like, I forgot. Like, my boyfriend tells me how much he likes it and like I put it on by habit."

"Go to the washroom and wash that stink off before I hose you down," demands Damballa.

Fern continues to whine, saying, "Like, I have it like on my clothes as well."

"I don't care if you have to take off your clothes and wash them. Just get rid of that horrible smell," yells Damballa.

77

"Like, can I like go home and change and like take a shower then?" Fern asks.

"No you can't go home. You have work to do here. Now maybe you will remember next time to not spray that nasty stuff on you when you're coming to work," snaps Damballa.

Fern stumbles off, bawling. Right behind her is another employee who is almost as round as Damballa. She has long brownish hair and also wears glasses, but they didn't make her eyes look big. She has this really dark blue color above her eyes and red, red color on her lips. She just continues to talk, even though nobody is paying attention to her.

"Zoelle what are you mumbling about?" Damballa says, irritated.

"I'm just telling Fern, 'I told her so,' and that she needs to hurry up so we can get to work," Zoelle replies.

"Zoelle, you need to quit being a know-it-all. Just close your mouth and get to your job of cleaning the kennels before people start showing up and leave Fern to me," Damballa yells.

"I'm just trying to help Ms. Damballa," replies Zoelle.

"Do you know what they call people like you, Zoelle? They call you a brown nosier or a busy body. Which one shall I call you?" Damballa asks.

"Neither. I'm neither one of those," Zoelle demands.

"You're both of those as well as a suck up, now be quiet and get to work. I don't want to hear another word out of you. And don't forget to check our little room back there and make sure it looks all pretty and that there are no dogs. Make sure all the medication and needles are out of sight and it doesn't smell. Spray Lysol if you have to," says Damballa.

"What's Fern going to be doing?" Zoelle asks.

"Don't worry about Fern. There you go being a busy body again. She is my problem. Just go do as I say," shrieks Damballa.

Now Damballa is walking around checking rooms to make sure everything is in order, as she has some people bringing in their Pit Bulls to her since the town has passed a law forbidding Pit Bulls in the city limits. Damballa says to herself, "Today a couple is bringing in their Pit Bull to me, just as I had planned with getting this law passed. Now I can destroy every last one of those evil creatures."

Fern approaches Damballa. Her hair is soaking wet and the kink is causing it to go every which way. Her clothes are also wet. The fog is gone.

"It took you long enough, now get back there and help Zoelle get things cleaned up. Guests will be arriving soon," Damballa yells.

"But I'm all wet," Fern says, whining.

"You'll dry eventually, so quit complaining and get to work," shouts Damballa.

"Yes Ms. Damballa and I'm sorry for upsetting you," Fern replies.

As Fern walks off, Damballa shakes her head and whispers, "So pathetic and to think she has a boyfriend. I bet he's a real winner."

Now the doorbell rings and Damballa walks quickly to the door. As she opens it, I see this big, beautiful, black and white male pit bull come walking in with a man and a woman. I also notice this dark circular mark on the top of his head in between his ears. I remember my mother has a mark like that.

I think to myself: *he sure does look familiar but I don't know from where.*

The woman is crying and asking the man, "Why can't we just move? I don't want to give him up."

"We have no choice. It's the law and we talked about this already. My job is here," says the man.

"You can find a job somewhere else where they allow Pit Bulls," cries the woman.

"No I can't. Besides Ms. LaVey is a very nice lady who loves Pit Bulls and will find him a wonderful home where he will be safe," explains the man.

As Damballa tries to convince them that she will take very good care of their dog she says, "Yes you don't need to worry, he is in very good hands."

She adds not quite under her breath, "Hands good at putting a needle in his leg"

"I don't trust her," cries the woman.

"It will be okay. She is not going to hurt him," replies the man.

Damballa starts to choke as he says this.

Now I know this is not a good place and this woman intends on killing this Pit Bull. I want to shout out, "Don't leave your boy here with this woman. She's evil, she is going to hurt him." But this is Miracle's vision and they can't hear me. I try anyway and shout, "No don't leave him, take him with you."

The couple keep petting the dog and the woman actually bends down and wraps her arms around his neck and gives him a kiss. The dog raises his head and licks her tears away. This only makes the woman cry even more. But I also notice that Damballa twitches her head when I shout out, that suggests to me that she hears me.

I yell, "I know what you are doing and I am going to stop you. You are not fooling me with your phony kindness." Again she jerks her head as if she hears me, trying to figure out where my voice was coming from.

"Now that you have said your goodbyes, let me take him back to a room and get him settled in," whispers Damballa.

She then turns to the couple and asks, "What is his name?"

The woman replies through her tears, "Gunner."

Gunner, I say to myself. *NO that can't be Gunner! That's my brother; she is going to kill my brother.*

Chapter Thirteen
The Three Rats

Damballa is walking Gunner down a long dark hallway. Gunner has a look on his face of pure fear. The temperature is getting colder and colder the closer they get to the end of the hallway. At the end of the hallway is a room where you can hear other dogs barking. She opens the door and there are about a half dozen Pit Bulls locked in small cages. Damballa yells, "Be quiet or I will get the needle now."

She opens a small cage and shoves Gunner in and locks the door. She only has three more cages to fill, then the fun will begin. She turns to leave the room and suddenly stops and looks down. There is a tiny little voice saying, "Damballa, down here. It's us, your brothers. We've been turned into rats."

I think to myself: *I knew I recognized those rats. I had wondered what became of them. So they are still around and up to no good.*

Damballa looks down and gasps. "How did this happen?" she asks.

They're standing in a dimly-lit corner, the three rats that Kiya had turned those three evil men into, the one with the long stringy blond hair, the other with the multicolored hair going in all directions, and the one with red hair. He still has the bandana on. All three of them looks the worse for wear. The one with the multicolor hair says, "We have been running and hiding from

81

cats. The dog that did this to us also had cats come after us. We have been running for days trying to get back here."

The dirty blond one says, "It was this Husky, she can talk and do magic. She has three other dogs with her, one is a Pit Bull. I think he is magical too. We were in an alley where we had trapped a Pit Bull to destroy and all of a sudden this Husky shows up out of nowhere. We thought we were going to be rich so we wanted to capture this talking dog, but before we knew it she turned us into these rats with cats chasing us."

"Are you going to stay rats forever?" Damballa asks.

The multicolored rat replies, "I hope not. It is not fun being a rat and being chased by cats."

"How do you get turned back?" Damballa asks.

The dirty blond rats says, "That answer lays with that Husky and Pit Bull. We need to set a trap. In our travels we were able to listen in on conversations. We found out that the Pit Bull that just came in, Gunner, came from the same puppy mill as the Pit Bull that is with the Husky. His name is Merlin. We think they might be brothers. We ran across a badger who works in this puppy mill and he was telling a story about a Husky that broke into his puppy mill and stole a Red Nose Pit Bull puppy by the name of Merlin. This badger is quite eager to get his paws on that Husky."

"This is great news. I can use Gunner to get the attention of this Husky and Pit Bull. I love when a plan just starts to come together. You know I'm not a fan of Pit Bulls, but a magical Pit Bull I can work with as long as he does what I say," shouts Damballa.

I now see the look on Damballa's face, as if she is remembering something.

"When I was with those people who brought Gunner in, I swear I could hear a voice telling me he knew what I was up to and that he was going to stop me. Do you think it was that Pit Bull and somehow he was able to see and hear me?" Damballa asks.

The multicolor haired rat says, "Since being turned into a rat, I believe anything."

"If that is true, then this might be easier than I thought," Damballa replies.

The red haired rat shouts, "We need to get our hands on that Husky so she can turn us back into humans and then turn her over to that badger. He is paying a pretty price for her. He wants her bad."

"Let me go back to my office and start putting the plan together. We will have to be very careful just in case those 'magical' dogs have the ability to hear us. We don't want them to know what we're planning. In the meantime, you three stay here where you're safe," Damballa explains.

The three rats are shaking their heads in agreement. The multicolored haired rat asks, "What about food?"

"Really, 'What about food?' You're lucky I don't go buy some traps that would snap your little necks," giggles Damballa.

The dirty blond rat squeaks, "But we're your brothers."

"Yes, who are so stupid that you got yourselves turned into rats. Now leave me alone so I can go to my office and think," bellows Damballa.

Damballa gets up and starts to walk out of the room and before opening the door, she reaches in her pocket a pulls out a couple of crackers that she had picked up earlier and throws them to the ground in the direction of the rats.

"There you go, eat on those for now," Damballa giggles.

The three rats look at each other and run toward the crackers.

Chapter Fourteen
The Trap is Set

All of a sudden we are back at Asgard with Rocky, Illusion, and Screech looking at us.

"What happened to you two?" Illusion asks.

"Miracle has visions of things that are currently happening or going to happen. I was seeing a woman who hates Pit Bulls and who is out to destroy all of us by taking Pit Bulls into her shelter and destroying them. One of them is my brother Gunner," I say anxiously.

"She sounds dreadful," replies Illusion.

"I need to talk to Kiya and we need to save them. Oh and Rocky, do you remember those three men that Kiya turned into rats?" I ask.

Rocky says laughing, "Yes, that was pretty funny."

"Well it turns out that those three rats are still running around and they happen to be this woman's brothers. They told her all about Kiya and how we are magical dogs. She is going to use Gunner to try and trap us. She is going to turn Kiya over to Turbo, who is looking for her to kill," I announce.

"And who is this Turbo?" Rocky asks.

"He's the badger who was at the puppy mill guarding us when Kiya came in and took me," I reply.

"A badger. They're mean and dangerous. This does not sound good," replies Rocky.

"No it doesn't. Is there anything I can do to help?" Illusion asks.

"Merlin's right. We need to find Kiya right away," says Screech.

"Leave that to me," says Illusion.

She starts shaking her train and the feathers come up in a fan around her. She shakes them two more times while closing her eyes and she is gone.

I ask while looking around, "Where did she go?"

"She went to find Kiya. Appears she found her location and went to get her. They should be back here any minute now," replies Screech.

"So she has more than one power?" I ask.

"She does, and so do most magical animals. It's just a matter of figuring out what they are and perfecting them," says Screech.

Just then Illusion appears with Kiya at her side.

"Before anyone says anything, just let me tell you that we have been aware of the situation at that shelter and with Damballa for some time. We were hoping to get you all trained in order to deal with this. You three just are not ready to fight the evil that lies within the walls of that shelter," explains Kiya.

"We must do something. She is going to kill my brother along with all the other Pit Bulls she has managed to get her hands on," I snap.

"This is what we were afraid of, that things would escalate to this point and lives would be lost," says Kiya.

"Not only is she going to start taking the lives of the Pit Bulls she has at the shelter, but she plans on capturing us to either do as she wants or she's going to destroy us. There's no telling what an evil human like her is capable of doing," Miracle replies.

"Exactly, we need to be smart and we must move very carefully, have a plan. I don't want anyone getting hurt or even killed," says Kiya.

I think to myself: *In the meantime my brother is suffering at the hands of this evil human. Somehow I need Miracle to have another vision so I can see what is going on.*

"Merlin, I can tell by the look on your face you are trying to come up with something. Trust me, we are all trying to come up with something but you have to promise me that you will not do anything without checking with me first, it's just too dangerous. Promise me!" Kiya demands.

I look at Kiya and say, "Okay, I won't do anything without checking with you first."

"Good, besides we have lost sight of her for now. She is up to something and before we just go charging in there, we need to know what we are up against and be prepared, understood?" ask Kiya.

All of us looked at Kiya and say, "understood."

"So in the meantime, my brother gets tortured and abused?" I ask.

"I know this has you upset and probably scared. We are working on it, but until we can locate her and determine what is going on, it's just too dangerous for any of us to go there. We have Elders working on it. We don't want anything to happen to Gunner either, or any of the other dogs she has," explains Kiya.

"So in the meantime?" I start to say but Kiya cuts me off.

"So in the meantime we wait. There are things around here that also need to be dealt with, classes to be taught, and training for the Celestial Animalympics to name a few," says Kiya.

"So that's that," snaps Miracle.

"Now that we have that settled for now, I need to get back to Mentor Purrcotta. We are still trying to determine if Rocky can participate in the running of the track at Celestial Animalympics, since he doesn't run but flies. Still can't get over that," says Kiya shaking her head.

"I don't see why that should disqualify him, just because his paws don't touch the ground," I mumble.

"That is not your concern. Remember what I said," says Kiya sternly.

Kiya turns and is walking away, then stops, looks back at us with raised eyebrows and squinted eyes, then turns back and continues walking away.

I look at Miracle and ask, "Do you think you can pull up another vision of that shelter so we can see what's going on?"

"Merlin, didn't you hear what Kiya said? It's too dangerous," shouts Illusion.

"Of course I heard what she said, but what can it hurt to just look?" I ask.

"I don't think you should be messing around with this. You're not trained enough," says Illusion, looking worried.

I have been practicing, besides we're just going to look. Well Miracle, what do you think?" I ask.

"I don't know. I can try. The ones I have had have just come to me. I have never tried to have a vision," replies Miracle.

"So you're willing to give it a try?" I ask.

"I'll try but I don't guarantee anything," Miracle says.

"Okay, you close your eyes and think about and picture that shelter in your head and I am going to stand right here with my paw on yours, so if something does happen I will be right here with you," I explain.

"I do not like this at all," says Illusion sounding worried.

"Don't worry it will be okay," I reply.

Now Miracle is closing her eyes and I put my paw on top of hers. Nothing happens for a while, then suddenly I see a dark cold room. It reminds me of the room at the puppy mill. I hear voices but don't see anyone. I can't make out what they were saying. I am thinking to myself: *I need to go there and see what is going on and make sure my brother is okay.* Now I feel my tail whipping around and around and now both Miracle and I are in this room.

Miracle opens her eyes and says, "How the heck did we get here?"

"I think I did it accidently. I was wishing I could be here to check on my brother and the next thing I know is that we're here," I reply.

"Are we here by ourselves?" says Miracle looking worried.

"I'm afraid so Miracle," I mutter.

"What do we do now?" asks Miracle.

"Let's walk around and see if anything is going on, but we need to be very quiet," I whisper.

We walk towards what looks like a door, then suddenly feel the floor under us moving and we begin to fall. I hit the ground hard and feel Miracle land next to me.

"What happened? Where are we? Are you okay?" asks Miracle.

"I hit pretty hard and I have some pain in my left front leg but I think it will be okay. I don't know but I think we might be in some trouble," I reply.

I look up to try and figure out how far down we are and if there is a way out. A light appears over the opening. It is Damballa.

"Look, I caught the magical Pit Bull and Rottweiler. Now I just need to get that Husky too," says Damballa excited

As I am watching Damballa I see three rat heads looking down at us laughing. I recognize them as the rats Kiya turned those men into. I hear one of them say, "You're going to have them turn us back into men before you do anything with them aren't you, Damballa?"

I hear Damballa laugh and say, "I don't know. I kinda like you three as rats."

I see her lift something like a gate over the top of the opening and then put a lock on it. I start barking and Miracle joins me.

Damballa leans over the opening and says, "Go ahead and BARK, make all the noise you want to. Nobody can hear you." She lets out a loud laugh. The hole we are in slowly goes dark again.

"Now what? I have to admit I'm feeling a bit nervous about our situation right now," says Miracle.

"I know me too. But remember, Rocky and Illusion was standing right there so hopefully they have gone for help. I can try to see if I can get the lock off that gate and move it but I still don't see a way out of this hole," I reply

"Well give it a try and maybe something will come to me or happen. I'm shooting for someone to come and get us. And what about our guardian? She is going to start to worry when she can't find us," says Miracle.

"I know, so we have to figure something out. Let me start with trying to get that lock off and move the gate," I reply.

I go into my playful bow, but the pain in my left front leg is making it difficult. I try pointing my tail straight up at the lock and gate. Closing my eyes I think to myself: *unlock the lock and move the gate, unlock the lock and move the gate.* I keep repeating this and slowly open my eyes. There is a bright green light coming from the end of my tail and aiming right at the lock and gate. I hear the lock and gate rattle.

"I think you are doing it, just keep going," says Miracle.

I don't respond to Miracle, as I'm trying to continue concentrating on opening the lock and moving the gate. Now I'm feeling my body start to shake from the pain in my left leg and the green light coming from my tail is fading, I don't hear the lock and gate rattling anymore and the hole is now dark again.

"What happened? Why did you stop?" Miracle asks.

"I didn't stop, but with the pain in my leg it is making it difficult to stay in my playful bow position, which made it stop by itself. I guess I need to practice more. I thought I could control it," I explain.

"Well this isn't a good time to figure that out, try again," Miracle snaps.

I go into my playful bow and again the pain in my leg continues but the green light comes out from the tip of my tail and I am aiming at the lock and gate. I can hear the lock and gate rattle, and then everything goes dark again.

"I think I need to rest my leg and try again later. I don't suppose you learned anything in that healing class that you can use to make my leg better?" I ask.

"No not really. I would hate to try and make things worse. So are you kidding me right now? We're just trapped down here in the dark and did I mention that's it is also cold!" shouts Miracle.

"Miracle, your getting mad at me right now is not going to help. We need to calm down and put our heads together and think of something. With all your complaining, what else can you do besides those visions? Anything?" I ask.

"Don't put this on me," Miracle shrieks.

"Let's try that thing that Mentor Na'vi was teaching us where we talk to each other with our minds and see if we can reach Rocky or Illusion," I suggest.

"Speaking of minds I think you have lost yours," blurts Miracle.

"WILL YOU JUST TRY IT," I yell.

"Okay, you don't need to yell at me. What do we do again?" asks Miracle.

"You think of Rocky, picture Rocky and in your mind tell him we are in trouble and to get help," I reply.

"Why do I have to do Rocky? Why don't you do Rocky?" asks Miracle with a whine.

"Please Miracle, stop arguing and just do it," I request.

"Alright, but if I am trying to reach Rocky, what are you going to be doing?" asks Miracle.

"I am going to try and reach Illusion and tell her the same thing," I reply.

"But why can't . . ." Miracle starts to say.

I cut her off and say, "Just do what I ask please."

I close my eyes and picture Illusion. In my mind I say, *Illusion I know you were there when we left. You saw what happened. Miracle and I are in big trouble. Damballa has us trapped in a hole that we can't get out of. I hurt my left leg when I fell into the hole. You need to get help right away. Go get Kiya and tell her what happened.* I just keep repeating that over and over hoping for a sign that she hears me.

All of a sudden out of nowhere, I hear Illusion's voice in my head saying, *I hear you Merlin and yes, I saw what happened. I'm getting Kiya. I was able to raise my train immediately after you two vanished so I have the trail to follow once I get more help.*

Hearing that, I lose my concentration and Illusion is gone.

"Miracle did you have any luck reaching Rocky?" I ask.

"To a point. He was confused as to where I was and how he was able to hear me. I just kept telling him to go for help and he kept asking, 'Get help for what?'" chuckles Miracle.

"It's okay. I was able to talk to Illusion and she is going to get Kiya. Illusion also said she was able to get the trail we took in her train so they will be able to find us," I explain.

"I don't understand how all that works but I am counting on you to get us out of here. So what do we do in the meantime?" asks Miracle.

"Let's just rest for now, because I have a feeling we are going to need all our strength for whatever is going to happen. Maybe my leg will start to feel better too. I can always try again later to see if I can get that lock off and move that gate," I reply.

"So we just sit here cold and in the dark for how long?" Miracle asks.

"Until help comes," I mutter.

"How long will that be?" Miracle asks.

"I don't know and you need to stop asking me all these questions because I do not have any answers for you," I snap.

"You don't have to be so mean about it," says Miracle.

I shake my head thinking: *don't respond. Just keep quiet. Maybe if you don't say anything, she will settle down.*

I find a dry spot and began to lay down to rest. As I'm closing my eyes and hear, "Merlin where are you? Where did you go?"

"I'm right here, Miracle. I am not going to leave you," I reply.

"Can I come lay next to you?" Miracle asks.

"Stay where you are, I will find you," I reply.

Of course she can't do what I ask and she starts wondering around until we bump into each other.

"Let's just lay here and rest until help comes." I mutter. Before I know it I hear Miracle snoring. I think to myself: *I'm glad one of us can sleep.* I curl up next to Miracle and my body is trembling, as I'm scared and wishing I was in the arms of my guardian and not in this cold dark hole. I close my eyes.

"Hey little Pit Bull, are you down there?" I hear.

I open my eyes and feel my body start to shake. That voice, I recognize that voice and I now feel a sense of fear come over me.

"What's wrong Merlin?" Miracle whispers, and then asks, "Who is that talking?"

"It's Turbo the badger. He's found me."

Chapter Fifteen
The Rescue

I feel Miracle jump up. She starts growling and barking.

"Why are you barking?" I ask.

"You said there is a badger up there. They're mean. I need to let him know that I'm mean too so he doesn't try anything," says Miracle.

"Let's just sit here for a minute and see what happens," I whisper.

"What do you think is going to happen?" asks Miracle.

"I don't know. I just need to think," I whisper.

"Think! Think about what? While we're sitting here waiting to see what happens and for you to think, they can be planning on killing us," snaps Miracle.

"Can you at least breathe so I know you are still alive down there? It would be a shame that I came this far to find you and you're already dead," shouts Turbo.

"Dead: did you hear him, Merlin? He wants us dead," gasps Miracle.

"NO, he wants me dead. He doesn't know about you. I don't think," I reply.

"Oh, that makes me feel so much better. Doesn't know about me but wants you dead," whispers Miracle.

"Miracle, we are going to be fine. Remember we have help on the way. Try to relax," I mutter.

I wish I could believe everything I am telling Miracle, but honestly I am scared to death.

"Did you see that, that glimmer of light?" asks Miracle.

"Good you saw it too. I thought I was seeing things. Let's just hope it's help and not the other," I reply.

We're sitting next to each other, then suddenly this ball of light comes floating down toward us. It hits the ground and the entire hole lights up. Miracle and I look at each other, then up and at the same time letting out a deep sigh of relief.

"I have never been so happy to see all of you, especially Rocky, as I am right now," yells Miracle.

Rocky, looking down at us, says, "Can I get that in writing."

"How did you get here? How did you find us? Did Illusion bring you here?" I ask.

Kiya then leans over the hole and says, "Rocky and Illusion got us here."

The look on Kiya's face is: *we're happy we found you and you are okay but you are in big trouble when we get out of here.*

"So Turbo isn't still up there? Did you see him?" I ask.

"No, Turbo isn't here. Are you trying to tell me that you saw him here?" asks Kiya.

"Yes, he was just there a minute ago," I reply.

"Oh, I can't wait to run into him. I owe him one," snaps Kiya as she looks down at her leg and see's the scare from where he had wounded her.

"Who else is with you?" I ask.

"I brought my friend Maagmen with us. I thought we could really use him. How is your leg, Merlin?" asks Illusion.

"Your leg, what happened to your leg?" asks Kiya.

"When we fell down in this hole, I landed on my left front leg pretty hard and I'm having trouble putting weight on it," I reply.

"I need you to find the center of the room and lay with your left leg up. I am going to try and fix it from up here," says Kiya.

"Okay, but I'm sorry, who is Maagmen?" I ask.

"You met him the same day you met me. He's the Adlet that was with me," answers Illusion

"I'm sorry the what?" I ask.

"Adlet: he is half man half dog and very strong," says Illusion.

"Yes, I remember now. Thank you Maagmen for coming to help us," I shout.

"No problem. I am up for some excitement," Maagmen shrieks.

"Can we take care of all the introductions and pleasantries after I fix your leg?" asks Kiya.

"Yes, sorry Kiya," I mutter. I think to myself: *great he's up for some excitement.*

"Are you in the center of the room?" Kiya asks.

"I think so, yes, I'm ready," I reply.

"Okay, you are going to see something like a lightning bolt heading toward your leg, don't move. It might sting but it won't be real painful," says Kiya.

For some reason her words were not a comfort to me. I see this flash of light heading toward my leg and prepare for the worst. It lands on my leg and I let out a yelp. Not that it hurt, but felt that a yelp was warranted.

"Did I get it on your leg," asks Kiya.

"Yes, once I saw it coming I moved just slightly to make sure it hit my leg," I reply.

"Did it hurt?" asks Miracle.

"It stung a bit but didn't hurt," I reply.

"Can you walk on it?" asks Kiya.

I get up and put some weight on it. It feels a little weird, but not painful. "Yes I can put weight on it. I think it is going to be alright," I shout.

"Then why did you yelp? You scared me. I thought what Kiya did hurt you more," snaps Miracle.

"I'm sorry. I guess it just startled me and I yelped. Can we quit talking about my leg now and think about getting out of here?" I ask.

"We need to get you two out of there first before we do anything else," Kiya says.

"OOPP, there's an idea," I whisper sarcastically. "I tried going into my playful bow and using my tail and I thought it was going to work but . . ."

Miracle cuts me off and yells, "As you can see, it didn't."

Kiya turns to Illusion and says, "From the looks of that lock and gate, I think it is going to take both of us to get that off. Are you up for it?"

"You just say when," says Illusions.

I see Kiya close her eyes as well as Illusion. Bright lights begin to circle above both Miracle and me. One of the lights lands on the lock and there is a small explosion and I see the lock falling to the ground next to me. Now several lights are moving, one lands on each corner of the gate and lifts it up and away. I feel a sense of relief.

Now what, how are we going to get out of here? I ask.

"Rocky, this is where you come in. Get those ears of yours flapping and go down there and get those two," Kiya explains.

"Are you sure you want me to do that?" asks Rocky.

"Huh, are you really sure you want him to do that?" Miracle asks.

"Unless you have another idea, yes I want him to do that," replies Kiya.

Miracle whispers to me, "They have to be kidding"

I whisper back, "He will do great."

"I know you need a running start to get those ears going, so just back up a little and run toward the hole," says Kiya.

"What if it doesn't work?" asks Rocky.

"Then you will end up down here with us," giggles Miracle.

I hear Rocky say, "Okay here goes nothing."

I continue to look up looking for Rocky then suddenly he is over the hole starting to fall and then his ears turn into bat wings and he lands next to us. He has a harness around him with a similar-looking device hanging off the other end of a rope that is attached to Rocky's harness.

"Now one of you climb into that harness and wait for Rocky to lift you out one at a time," says Kiya.

"Can I go first?" asks Miracle.

"Just make sure you have that harness all the way on and just sit there and let me lift you out, RELAX!" says Rocky.

Miracle is sliding the harness on with the help of some magic and when she is completely in says, "Okay, I'm ready."

Rocky starts flapping his ear and rises up slightly and says, "Okay Miracle here we go."

I sit there watching Rocky start flying toward the top. As he goes, the rope starts getting tighter. Once it got to the point of lifting Miracle up it jumps a little. I can see him struggling with her weight. I then see Rocky come back down some, then with what looks like everything he has, those ears really start flapping harder and lifts Miracle up and out of the hole.

"Get ready Merlin, he is coming for you next," Kiya says.

"I'm ready," I reply.

I'm sitting patiently looking for Rocky, worrying that something happened but then here he comes flying down to get me.

"Had a little problem getting Miracle out of the harness, seems it didn't want to let go of her . . . Are you in the harness good and tight and ready to go?" asks Rocky.

"I am ready. A little nervous but ready to get out of this hole," I mutter.

Rocky starts flapping his ears and rises again slightly and says, "Here we go Merlin, let's get out of here."

He is lifting me out of that hole and sits me next to Kiya. She helps me get out of that harness and untangles me from the rope. I look at Kiya and know I'm in big trouble when we got back to Asgard.

Kiya says to Illusion, "Fill in that hole just to make sure one of us doesn't end up back down there."

Illusion raises her train and gives it three good shakes, the hole starts filling itself in.

"Can we get out of here and back to Asgard now?" asks Miracle.

"No. Since we are here we need to save my brother and all those other dogs she has locked back there to kill," I shout.

"I was afraid you were going to say that," sighs Miracle.

"I think we need to go down this hall," I mutter.

"Illusion and Rocky, you stay here in case there is trouble and if we are not back here in fifteen minutes, something went wrong. Merlin, Miracle and Maagmen, come with me. We need to be quiet but also get in and out as quickly as possible," explains Kiya.

We walk down the hall, standing very close to each other. I see a light coming from under one of the doors.

"I don't think it is that one. From what I remember from Miracle's vision, Damballa was taking my brother further back and the room was dark," I whisper.

"Okay let's keep going. I think I am picking up on the scents of canines," says Kiya.

We continue past several doors before Kiya stops. It is very dark and cold. We stand there to let our eyes adjust to the darkness. I can finally see the others.

"I am going to open the door. Everyone make a quick scan around the room to make sure we are in the right place. If we are, we need to get in and get those cages open and get the dogs as fast as we can," says Kiya.

Kiya opens the door slowly and we walk into the room as carefully as we can in the dark. Suddenly a light comes on and I hear a woman yell, "NOW." A canvas-type netting falls from the ceiling and lands on all of us. Damballa and two other women are there tying the thing down. We're trapped.

An excited Damballa says, "We got them, it worked. Look, we even got the Husky that badger is wanting. We're going to make plenty off her. What in the world is that thing?" She points at Maagmen.

"What? Haven't you ever seen a half man half dog before? I bet not and when I get loose you are going to wish you had not seen one now," Maagmen yells.

Damballa says laughing, "You think you're going to get loose, do you? I put a lot of thought into this and did research on how to capture magical creatures. You're not going anywhere."

"And you are not going to make a fortune on that Husky either. You'll be lucky if I let you out of here alive," says Turbo.

"You must be the badger that's been looking for the Husky and Pit Bull. As you can see, I now have them," shouts Damballa.

I think to myself: *we are really in trouble now. At least before I knew Kiya could help us but now she is trapped with us and Turbo is here.*

"You don't want to take me on Damballa, you will lose. Just let me have the Husky and the Pit Bull. Whatever you do with the rest of them is up to you," says Turbo.

Now Turbo is in Damballa's face and they are eye ball to eye ball. I don't know what Damballa saw in Turbo's eyes, but whatever it was scared her and she backs away from him.

"Fine, you take the Husky and the Pit Bull," snaps Damballa.

"Great, now that we have settled that let me get them and be on my way," shouts Turbo.

"I'm not going with you and I'm not staying here either. I'm going to get my brother and we are getting out of here," I holler.

Turbo and Damballa start laughing.

"A Pit Bull with a sense of humor. Too bad I'm going to kill him," chuckles Turbo.

I hear Miracle growling and barking. I look at Kiya to see some sort of hope in her eyes but there is none. Now I'm thinking: *wait a minute we still have Illusion and Rocky. I almost forgot about them. Everyone else must have forgot about them too.*

This netting they have over us is so tight we can't move. I look around and see dogs in cages that have moved to the furthest corner of their cage to avoid any harm that may come their way. I continue to look around the room and I see him: Gunner. They have him in chains that are around his neck and all four legs. He looks weak and very thin. I also see wounds that were not there when that couple turned him over to Damballa. Now I am feeling angry and start to growl.

The skinny girl with dirty hair says, "Oh, like, he is so cute, can't I just like keep him?"

"What is wrong with you, Fern? I knew you weren't very smart but not to this degree," snaps Damballa.

"What are you going to do with that ugly thing?" the heavyset women says, pointing at Maagmen.

"I don't know who you are calling ugly but have you looked in the mirror? You have to be one of the ugliest humans along with your friends over there that I have ever seen," says Maagmen.

The heavyset women replies, "Are you kidding? Me, ugly?"

"Ugly beyond belief," chuckles Maagmen.

Before the arguing could continue, Damballa yells, "Zoelle be quiet. You never know when to just shut up."

The three rat brothers appear and go over to Kiya and one of them says, "You, Husky, you need to turn us back to the way we were before that badger takes you."

Kiya looks down at the three rats and says, "Oh, look what the cat dragged in, three rats. So you didn't become dinner for my cat friends."

Damballa's eyes become very wide and she says, "You do speak. I didn't believe it but now I am hearing you for myself. Too bad I have to turn you over to the badger, I would become very rich otherwise. Do you know what people will pay to hear a talking dog? Come on Turbo, let me at least keep the Husky."

"There is no point in keeping me because I won't help make you rich and I will not speak, so you will be made a fool. Everyone will think you are crazy," snarls Kiya.

"Oh you will speak when I need you to trust me. I have my ways," snaps Damballa.

One of the rats says, "But what about the badger? That is not a creature you want to make mad. He is dangerous."

"Yes, what about the badger, did you forget I was here? Now enough of all this talk, I'm taking the Pit Bull and Husky NOW!" yells Turbo.

Damballa raises her right arm and in her hand is a gun. "I think this will stop you as well as everyone of you, so you better do as I say if you don't want to get hurt or end up dead," snaps Damballa.

My mind is going a million miles a minute trying to figure out how we are going to get out of this and if we are all going to make it out alive. I can't help it, but my body is trembling and shaking. Kiya sees me and inches her way over to me to try and offer some kind of comfort. She puts her paw on mine and says, "Merlin we are going to be fine." I wish I could believe her but I am scared.

"Turbo, you come with us," Damballa points the gun at him and says. "Let's leave them here just like this for now, at least this way I know they won't be escaping this time and I need to go to my office and figure out my next move."

"You better think about what I am going to do to each of you when I get out of here," Maagmen replies.

Damballa, still pointing the gun at Turbo, turns and walks out of the room, turning off the lights, closing and locking the door.

"Gunner can you hear me? It's me, Merlin. Are you okay?" I ask.

"A bit beat up and hungry, but for now I am okay. Wait did you say Merlin, as in my brother?" Gunner asks.

"Yes. Where is mom and our sisters?" I ask.

"I will tell you everything once we get out of here. How did you find me?" asks Gunner.

"My friend Miracle has visions and she picked up on this evil place and I watched your people bring you in here and leave you, believing you were going to a great home," I reply.

"This is as far as I got. There is no great home. Damballa lied to my owners so they would bring me here so she could kill me," says Gunner.

"That's not going to happen. We still have two friends we left down the hall a ways. If we're not back in fifteen minutes, they will come looking for us," I reply.

"So we better be ready and since none of us can move much, we might as well rest so we will have all our strength to battle these evil humans when the time comes," says Kiya.

I'm laying next to Kiya and close my eyes. I am seeing my guardian outside playing with us as we all rolled around in the grass and chased each other. We all look so happy. I wake with a startle from the sound of a crash. I realize I am only dreaming. I am still in this nightmare. But what was that crash, I wonder.

I lift my head as much as I can and try to see toward the door. At first I think I am seeing things. I blink my eyes a couple of times and standing in the door way is Illusion and Rocky. Now I hear Damballa and those other humans coming back our way. I whisper, "You two need to hide so they don't trap you."

Illusion and Rocky move to a corner toward the back of the room out of sight. Damballa, with Turbo still in front of her, comes storming in.

"How did this door get opened? Damballa turns and looks at Fern and Zoella. "Did one of you two idiots open this door?" Damballa asks.

"Was it you Fern, wanting to keep that red nosed Pit Bull?" asks Zoella.

"No like I haven't been back here," Fern replies.

Maagmen speaks up and says, "Yes it was her. She thought she could sneak the Pit Bull out without anyone noticing."

"No I didn't he's, like, lying," screams Fern.

"It doesn't matter right now. I will deal with that later. At least I got back here before any harm was done," says Damballa.

They turn and start to walk out of the room and I hear a voice say, "Not so fast."

Damballa turns back around and there stands Illusion with her train up staring Damballa in the eye and shaking her train at them. A mist comes out from her feathers and circles the humans. She puts them in a trance. Damballa drops the gun and Turbo runs out the door.

"Why didn't that work on Turbo?" I ask.

"Only a certain kind of magic works on other animals with powers," replies Illusion.

"So he is still out there and just as dangerous?" I ask.

"I'm afraid so. But we need to get out from under this netting before we can do anything," replies Kiya.

"I need all of you to get into the middle of that net so I can start to try and remove it from on top of you," says Illusion.

"Come work on this corner first so I can try to help," Maagmen replies.

Illusion walks over to the corner closest to Maagmen. She lowers her train and turns her back to the corner.

"Are you all ready, Maagmen?" asks Illusion.

"I'm ready," Maagmen replies.

Illusion starts shaking her train and Maagmen grabs the corner with his bare hands and starts pulling. I can see the net moving. I say to myself: *please let this work*, over and over again. I see the corner where Maagmen and Illusion are give way. Illusion moves to the next corner now that the one corner is off. Maagmen moves to the next corner to help.

"We just need to get this corner loose, then everyone can crawl out," shouts Maagmen.

I feel the other corner come loose and I am able to move. I climb out from under the net and everyone else climbs out right behind me.

"We need to get these dogs out of these cages," I yell.

"I'll go to the office and see if I can't find information on these dogs and start making calls to have their owners come get them," says Maagmen.

"You first need to call 911 and get the authorities here and if you have time, then look for the owner's information. Otherwise the authorities can contact them. We don't want them finding us," explains Kiya.

"What about my brother?" I ask.

"Let's just get everyone out of these cages and out of this room, then we can figure everything out," Kiya replies.

"Okay, let me go call that 911 number and get things rolling," says Maagmen.

Kiya is going around using her tail and unlocking all of the cages. I'm right behind her, using my paws and nose to open the doors.

"Let's have them go out back where it is fenced. We can all use some fresh air after being locked in these cages and in that room," Gunner suggests.

Just then I hear Maagmen say, "Hold on, we have a problem."

We all turn to look and there in the doorway stands Maagmen with Turbo standing right behind him holding the gun Damballa dropped when Illusion had put her in that trance.

"Nobody is going anywhere. I have about had all I can take of this. I was to just come in and get you two and leave, which is exactly what I'm going to do right now," announces Turbo.

Turbo pushes Maagmen back into the room with us and motions for Kiya and me to come toward him.

"What are you going to do with us?" I ask, trying to hide my fear.

"I am going to kill you just like I did your mother and as for the Husky, well I'm going to enjoy torturing her after all the trouble she caused for me with my master," snarls Turbo.

"What do you mean you killed my mother? My mother is dead?" I ask. Now I feel the fear leave and anger take over.

"Well let's just say I left her for dead," Turbo says, laughing.

As I stand there looking at Turbo I can feel something stirring inside me. I have never felt this before. My tail is now feeling heavy. For some reason I yell, "Everybody get down." I feel the need to go into my playful bow. I still feel so much anger toward Turbo. My tail now aims itself toward Turbo. I see Turbo drop the gun and come up on his back legs and point his long claws at me. I feel my tail jerk, and then a bolt of light comes shooting out of my tail and hits the wall next to Turbo and explodes.

"Oh, so you want to play do you?" asks Turbo.

With his claws pointing right at me I see a bolt of light heading my way and I'm able to move just in time. It hits one of the cages behind me, sending it crashing to the ground. That brought back memories of being at the puppy mill with my mother, brother and sisters. I can feel my tail starting up again. It aims for Turbo. He is aiming for me at the exact same time. Bolts of light come sailing from both of us and they end up crashing together right in front of us and explode . I hear someone ask, "Merlin, are you okay?"

"I'm good," I shout.

"Well that's too bad. Let me try again," snaps Turbo.

Before he can get another round off, I'm able to get my tail aimed at him again and send another round at him. I hear a cry in pain coming from Turbo. Someone yells, "I think Merlin got him."

Then Kiya comes out of nowhere and says, "I owe you this one."

Before Kiya can get into position, Turbo turns his attention toward Kiya and says, "I don't think so, you're mine." And a bolt of light hits Kiya and she lets out a loud cry.

"Kiya, no not Kiya," I yell.

"What's a matter Merlin? Afraid I killed Kiya the way I killed that Rottweiler that was pretending to be your mother? What was her name? Mikayla right?" asks Turbo.

Now I can really feel the anger inside of me. "You killed Mikayla? Now you need to pay, she deserves justice," I shout.

I get into my playful bow and aim my tail at Turbo and scream, "This is for Mikayla and my mother."

"Not this time Pit Bull," replies Turbo.

I watch as the bolt of light from my tail is heading toward Turbo. He claps his front claws together and disappears right before it is going to hit him and hits the wall again, exploding. I hear the gun go sliding across the floor. I pick up the gun in my mouth and go to find Kiya. She is laying on her side. I see blood coming from her shoulder. I lay the gun down next to her.

Kiya, are you alright? I ask

"I'll be fine once we get back to Asgard. I'm afraid I'm not going to be much help right now though" Kiya replies.

"That's okay, we can handle it and get everyone out. Gunner, Gunner where are you?" I ask.

"I'm right here. Are you okay Merlin? I can't believe you found me. I thought I was going to die in here and never see any of my family again," says Gunner.

I can feel some tears swelling up in my eyes as I look at Gunner and say, "You do look a bit like mom. You have her eyes and the same marking in between your ears like she did."

"Like she does. I don't think she is dead, so you have to find her and our sisters," says Gunner as he walks over to me and licks my tears. "You always were the baby."

I sniffle and shake my head and say, "Let's get everyone out of here. Gunner you lead the way."

Everyone is out of the cages and they are following Gunner to a door. Gunner raises his two front paws up and hits the bar on the door as hard as he can and the door flies open and everyone runs outside.

"I am going to go find Maggmen and see if he needs anything," says Illusion.

"I want to go with you. I have an idea on a punishment for these humans," I reply.

Illusion and I find Maagmen on the phone. He is saying, "You need to get police and whoever else over to the MGAS. It's an emergency. You should also alert the City Council to get over here too."

I tell Illusion my idea and she agrees with my punishment and says she will take care of it. I then go outside to talk with my brother.

"Gunner, I want you to come back to Asgard with me. You will be safe there and never have to worry about being used to fight or as a bait dog ever again," I explain.

"I didn't have to worry about that with my new owners, they took me from that dog fighting place. It wasn't until they came up with this BSL law and made everyone with a Pit Bull turn them into this shelter that I was placed in danger," replies Gunner.

"What does BSL stand for?" I ask.

"It's stands for Breed Specific Legislation, it's for all the bully breeds. Humans created this law to discriminate against us. A lot of humans have convinced other humans that we are dangerous, aggressive and can't be trusted. They are using this law to destroy us. This is a law that Damballa created and was able to get the town people and city council to support in order to get all the Pit Bulls turned over to her so she could destroy us. I think this law is spreading around the world, so it's not just here that they are destroying dogs because of this stupid law," says Gunner.

"You don't want to come with me?" I ask.

"I love my humans. They made a mistake. I want to go home with them. But you have to promise you will come visit me from time to time," says Gunner.

"I promise. Now tell me about mom," I reply.

Gunner tells me the story of what took place at the puppy mill after I was taken and how he and my two sisters were sold to a dog fighting ring. My sisters are there to produce puppies and are kept in really bad conditions. He heard the head of the puppy mill tell Turbo to get rid of our mom.

"Do you think Miracle can try to have a vision to help you find our mom and sisters?" asks Gunner.

"Maybe, but we need to get everyone here taken care of first," I reply.

Maagmen finds a blanket and we all go to where Kiya is laying. Maagmen helps her get on the blanket. We all grab a piece of the blanket to carry her out of the building, leaving the gun inside. She is still bleeding, but awake.

"What did you do with the dogs, Gunner and the humans?" asks Kiya.

"We left Gunner and the dogs that were in the shelter in the backyard with plenty of food and water. As for the humans, Merlin came up with a brilliant plan to use similar devices that humans have been using on us for years as a punishment," replies Miracle.

The police, the city council and a bunch of important-looking people in suits are walking toward the building. Once inside they find their way to Damballa's office, where they find Damballa and her two humans tied up with collars around their necks that has a box on it with two prongs that touch the skin at their throats. We hide outside in some bushes to watch.

The authorities, police and city council look surprised at what they see. They then notice the note we left that says, "These people have been misleading you folks. Damballa perceives a Pit Bull in particular as a vicious breed that is evil and believes they have lots of aggression in their genes and needs to be destroyed. When people hate things they tend to get a passion built up inside. So she created this law so whoever owns a Pit Bull would bring it to her and she would kill it. What she doesn't understand is that good dogs under the control of bad people do bad things. The Pit Bulls in the backyard are her latest victims. Please contact their owners and have them come get their dog. As for the BSL, it needs to end.

"You will notice collars around the human's necks. You won't be able to remove them. These are for a punishment that fits the crimes they have committed against the Pit Bull Breed. To keep them from shocking these humans, they will have to clean kennels and bathe dogs every day for eight hours until it is felt they have learned their lesson.

"We would like you to keep this facility open for animals in need, but the name needs to be changed to Pets Safety Alliance and no animal will ever face being euthanized, abused or hungry as long as they are in this facility. To finish up, if any one of them has a thought about abusing another animal the collar will correct them with a shock.

"We will be watching!!!"

The man in a suit reading the letter says, "That's all it says. It isn't signed. I wonder who is watching." He takes a quick glace around the room to see if there is someone there he doesn't know and notices the gun on the floor and picks it up and puts it in his jacket. He then shrugs his shoulders and says, "Let's get these dogs owners called and get these dogs home." He points to a policemen and says, "Put these three in your car and take them downtown. Once I get done with all their charges, they will be lucky if they ever get out of jail."

I can hear Damballa's two humans crying and blaming each other for the trouble they are in. I feel sad that my brother isn't coming with me but at the same time happy that he is going back to the home and people he loves. All of us meet at the side of the building now that those three have been taken away and the dogs in the backyard are being taken care of.

"I think we are all ready to get back to Asgard. I know I am," Kiya announces.

"I know I am too and to get home to my guardian," I reply.

"Everyone stand in a circle together around me," says Kiya.

Then I hear a tiny voice say, "What about us?"

It's the three rats. Miracle says, "What about you? I'm surprised you're still here."

One of the rats asks, "Aren't you going to turn us back?"

"After the role you were playing in there with those dogs and us getting captured, NO I am not turning you back and you better scram before I call those cats again," snaps Kiya.

The three rats take off running. We are standing in a circle around Kiya. Illusion raises her train and starts shaking it. I now feel relaxed knowing I'm heading back to Asgard. As we are leaving the shelter, I see one extra critter jump in at the last minute and come with us: THAT RAT.

Chapter Sixteen
Back at Asgard

We are still in a circle around Kiya as we all enter back into Asgard. I feel something running around my paws. Others are saying, "Did you feel that?" "What was that?" I look around to try and see what it is and I catch a glimpse of it running away. It is one of those rats, the one with the multicolored fur.

I yell, "I just saw it out of the corner of my eye. It's that multicolored furry rat. I thought I saw it jump in at the last minute. What do we do?"

"First you need to get me to the infirmary so I can get this wound taken care of. I will let the rest of the Elders and Mentors know to be on the lookout for it. We might even have to set a trap or two to catch it. We do not need something like that running around Asgard," says Kiya.

"I know I am ready to get back to the Sugar Ranch and to my guardian. I have had way too much excitement and want to just have something to eat and go to bed," I reply.

"I think we all feel that way but if I can have just another minute of your time before you go, I want to talk to you all about what we just went through. We are all very lucky that I was the only one that got hurt. Not everyone was really trained to go to that dangerous place and deal with such dangerous people. I am just thankful that everyone made it out okay. What if one of you three would have been hurt or even worse killed? How would your guardian react to that? I know you thought you were doing the right thing but this can NEVER happen again. Miracle, Merlin do you hear me?" Kiya asks.

We're both standing there shaking our heads and then I think of something to say.

I start to say, "But" and before I can get anything further out, Kiya snaps, "But nothing. And I don't want to hear another word. Now as long as we all have a clear understanding I think it is time for you three to get back to your guardian and I will see you tomorrow."

I say again, "But—"

"What is it Merlin? What haven't I made crystal clear?" asks Kiya.

"Nothing, but what about finding my mother? I need to find her," I reply.

"Not today. I heard what your brother told you about her and I promise you we will do everything we can to find not only your mother but your sisters but we can't do it today. Now you need to go. From what I am being told, your guardian has been looking for you for a while now," says Kiya not looking very well.

"Come on Merlin, let Kiya go get her wound taken care of and Maagmen and I will walk you back to the dog house," says Illusion.

I say to Illusion as we walk, "You do understand that I must find the rest of my family. They are with evil people."

"Yes, Merlin we all understand. But didn't you learn anything from what we just went through?" asks Illusion.

"Yes I know but I am just worried about them," I reply.

"From what Kiya was saying you need more training so you don't put yourself and others in danger. I'm getting used to you being around and want to keep it that way," Illusion replies.

"Really, you like having me around?" I ask.

"No, that is not what I said, I'm getting used to you being around is what I said," responds Illusion.

"Well here we are and I hear our guardian already calling for us," says Rocky.

"I do too. We better get going," I reply.

Maagmen sticks out his hand and says, "I have to admit you did bring excitement back into my life, almost too much. See you tomorrow."

I stick my paw out and he grabs it with his hand and we shake with Miracle's and Rocky's paws as well. I see Miracle giving Maagmen kind of a side grin and I start to giggle.

"What are you giggling at?" asks Miracle.

"Nothing, absolutely nothing. Illusion will I see you tomorrow?" I ask.

"Yes if you're lucky," Illusion says. As she turns to walk away, I can hear her purring and starting to shake her train at me. I also see that her feathers are changing from a dark bluish purple to a maroon red. I am not sure what that means, but watching her change color like that makes me feel happy.

Rocky and Miracle are almost through the doghouse. I start running to catch up to them. Our guardian is running around the Ranch looking for us almost in a panic when she spots us.

Almost in tears she says, "Where have you three been? I have been worried sick about you. I couldn't find you anywhere."

She sits down on the lawn and calls for all three of us to come to her. We run up to her and as we get close, she starts tapping her leg. All of us are trying to find a place to lick and to let her know we are okay. I am able to get a tear or two.

"Okay enough of this, but I could ring each one of your necks for scaring me like that," shouts our guardian.

I think: *Scared, you have no idea.*

We walk up to the house and our guardian holds the door open for us. She already has our dinner ready and sets it down for us. We all finish our meal and find a place where we can cuddle up and go to sleep. As I drift off, I can still hear the TV and feel my guardian kissing my head and rubbing my back.

TO BE CONTINUED!